Miracles Can Dream

A Novel

J.J. Francesco

When Miracles Can Dream

Copyright © 2022 J.J. Francesco

No part of this work may be reproduced in any form or by any electronic or mechanical means, including information storage and retrieval systems, without written permission in writing from the author, except brief quotations for review purposes. This book is a work of fiction. Names, characters, places, and incidents are either the product of the author's imagination or are used fictitiously, and any resemblance to actual persons, living or dead, business establishments, events, or locales is entirely coincidental.

Book and cover design by Jansina

The text is set in "Libre Baskerville."

The display type is "Adobe Handwriting Tiffany" (TJ), "Adobe Handwriting Ernie" (Micah), and "Viktor Script" (Title and all other instances).

ISBN: 978-1-63522-026-1

Printed in the United States of America

10   9   8   7   6   5   4   3   2   1

RIVERSHORE BOOKS

Rivershore Books
8982 Van Buren St. NE • Minneapolis, MN 55434
763-670-8677 • info@rivershorebooks.com

Dedication

For Jesus, Mary, & Joseph: The Holy Family.
The Heart of Christmas and Model for All Families.

"Santa Claus is anyone who loves another
and seeks to make them happy;
who gives himself by thought or word or deed
in every gift that he bestows."

–Edwin Osgood Grover

Chapter 1
TJ

I stopped believing in Santa Claus the night they died.

It was four years ago on Christmas Eve. I was six and a half, and I couldn't wait to open my presents.

I wrote to Santa ten times that year to ask him for a special Pikachu. It could wiggle and run just like Pikachu did on TV. Only he couldn't use Thunderbolt for real. Just the sound effects.

Mom took me and my sister Melanie to my great aunt's house for dinner. I never saw Aunt Phyllis except at Christmas time. She was Mom's aunt and lived in a big house in the upper part of the county with lots of farms. It doesn't snow much down here, but somehow there was always snow on the ground for Christmas Eve where she lived.

I wore my special Christmas suit. Red tie, green vest, and a cheesy snowman pin from Grandma that played three different songs.

Melanie had just turned four. She had a brand-new green dress that everyone there loved. There was a Mannheim Steamroller song playing on the radio when we arrived. Melanie didn't even wait to go inside before she started dancing. She loved dancing and would dance to anything, even commercials on TV. But her dress twirling when she danced to soft

Francesco

Christmas music is still something I see anytime I close my eyes.

Dad didn't go with us that year. He had to stay late to manage the store. It was Christmas Eve, after all. Customers had last-minute shopping to do and he couldn't leave his crew just so he could go to a party. Of course, the store closed at 4 o'clock, so I never did get why he couldn't come with us. But I didn't question Dad.

Aunt Phyllis had the highest, most screechy voice I ever heard. Before we even got into the house, I could hear her shouting, "Is that My CJ?" She never could get my name right.

My parents named me after Mom's dad, my grandfather who died before I was born. His name was Theodore James Callahan. He didn't have any sons so Mom wanted to honor him and give me the same name. I never really liked the name Theodore, though. Too long. Since I can remember, everyone always called me TJ. Except Dad. He called me Theo. And Aunt Phyllis. She called me every other nickname possible. CJ. BJ. EJ. AJ. JJ. Even ZJ once. But never TJ. I never knew if she did it on purpose or if she was just old and forgetful. But she usually slipped me five dollars whenever I saw her. So she could call me whatever she wanted.

"Santa already came and put gifts for both of you under the tree," she said as she led us into the house. Her tree was only a little taller than me, but it had

When Miracles Can Dream

so many lights and ornaments on it that you could barely see any tree at all. There were tons of presents underneath it, all the same size and shape, and all wrapped in the same Santa Claus wrapping paper.

Other relatives whose names I don't remember came in to say "Hi" to Mom and tell Melanie and me how big we'd gotten.

It always smelled the same too. Oil frying. Aunt Phyllis was Italian and so every Christmas Eve she fried fish. Lots of fish. They said there were seven, but I think there were more. She made flounder and shrimp and weird gooey black things and fish with really crazy names. None of us kids ever ate any of them. Gross.

But we did eat the fried dough. It was weird and lumpy stuff that was crispy and chewy and really, really good. Sometimes they even put sugar on it. I usually ran to grab a piece and Mom would tell me not to eat too many so I didn't spoil my dinner. Like I would eat any of the fish anyway.

After dinner and dessert, everyone gathered in the family room while one of the old people told stories from when everyone was younger while *A Christmas Story* played on the TV without the sound. Most of the kids usually played games or something, but I always listened because hearing about Mom or Grandma or Aunt Phyllis when they weren't so old was funny. Sometimes I tried to imagine Mom when she was my age or what I'd look like if I were as tall as Dad. Maybe having everyone listen to me tell stories about when I was a kid.

After the grownups ran out of stories, we all opened the gift Aunt Phyllis got everyone. That year, it was some snow globe that played the same three songs as my snowman pin. Inside it was a church and kids running around. It snowed inside when you shook it. For a moment, I wondered what it would be like to live at the north pole and what Santa's Christmas celebrations must be like. Did Santa give gifts to all the elves too?

I don't remember how late it was when we left. Just that Aunt Phyllis kept saying how it was a shame my dad couldn't come and telling Mom to drive safe and to call her in the morning. Melanie fell asleep on the way home, clutching Talulah, the weird plush doll she dragged everywhere. We kept our snow globes in a bag in the trunk and Mom drove us home.

I remember driving past downtown with all the old buildings and Christmas lights everywhere. White lights. Red lights. Green Lights. Blue lights. Wrapped around buildings and strung over the street. The Church had a big Nativity Scene on the lawn and all the stores had Santas and Snoopy and Buddy the Elf and others in the window. For one moment, it all felt like I was in the snow globe Aunt Phyllis gave us. I even thought I saw Santa passing for a second.

When we got home, Mom made us quickly change into our pajamas. We got new ones every year, and they were the only gift Mom let us open on Christmas Eve. She always matched them so we'd all have the same ones. This year's were red and black checker patterned. Melanie seemed to like them, but I thought they were kind of hot and itchy. I figured I could take them off once Mom tucked me into bed and put them back on in the morning before we woke her up. As long as I had them on for Mom's pictures.

Mom turned on "Silent Night" by Mannheim Steamroller and took out her camera to video Melanie and me hanging up our stockings. It took over ten minutes for us to actually do it since Mom asked Melanie and me questions. We all knew the answers to each one of them. *What did you ask Santa to bring you for Christmas? Have you been good all year? Are you ready to go to sleep? What if Santa comes and sees you're still awake?*

Every so often, I could see her looking toward the door. Probably checking to see if Dad was coming home. He didn't come home that night.

After Melanie did a dance and ran around the whole house for some reason, we finally got to hang up our stockings by the fireplace. This year we had brand new bigger stockings that we all used glue and glitter to write our names on. Well, Mom did Melanie's because she couldn't spell. But I learned how to spell my name all the way back in preschool, so I could do it all by myself.

Francesco

After the stockings were hung, Melanie and I ran up to bed and waved goodnight to the camera. Mom came up after and went into Melanie's room to kiss her goodnight. Then came into mine. "Merry Christmas, TJ," she said as she closed my door.

I turned on my side and tried to fall asleep, but I was too excited to play with the Pikachu Santa was going to bring me. But I knew Santa would only come if I was asleep, and I didn't want him to turn back. So I got out of bed, threw my PJs on the floor, and turned on the radio to try and see if that helped. They were playing a song about Mommy kissing Santa Claus and I laughed at how silly it was to think of Mom kissing Santa when she could barely kiss Dad in front of us.

As I crawled back under the covers, I heard a weird rumbling sound, but I didn't know what it was.

Then I was in a Pokémon battle using Pikachu and Mewtwo. I was just about to win when Santa woke me up.

I yanked open my eyes and saw a pink sky above me. A freezing wind whipped against my face. I could see Santa standing above me. "Shhh, it's going to be alright."

I tried to get up, but he held me back down. Then I realized I was coughing like crazy.

I only had on an undershirt and my underwear so every part of me was shivering. My pajamas must've still been on the floor in my room. But why did Santa take me outside?

I looked over at my house. It didn't look any different, but I saw people running in and out of it dressed like doctors.

One of them put something on my face that blew a lot of air down my throat. It was weird at first, but then it helped me stop coughing. I looked over and saw Melanie on the ground next to me. Her eyes were closed and a lady dressed like the others was pressing down on her chest and sweating a lot. I wondered why she was sweating when it was so cold out.

Then I saw them bringing Mom out of the house on a bed on wheels. I tried to call to her, but someone's hands held me back.

I looked up and saw Santa again. He was crying too. Then I felt wheels under me rolling. I was on a bed on wheels too. Santa got farther and farther away until I couldn't see him anymore. I looked over and saw them zipping up Melanie into a long bag. Why were they doing that? How was she supposed to breathe in that?

Then they rolled me toward a big ambulance with blinking lights that were so bright, I couldn't see the Christmas lights anymore.

I felt something cold on my head. A snowflake? Then the doors slammed shut.

Francesco

I opened my eyes and saw Dad. His big blue eyes were looking down on me and I could see him smiling. Usually his smiles looked fake. This time, I could see he really was happy to see me.

"Hey, Theo. Good to see you up." He stroked my hair. "You really scared me."

"I did?" I looked around the room. It was a hospital room. There wasn't any sign of Christmas anywhere. Then I heard something next to me. *Beep. Beep.* My heartbeat!

That air tube under my nose was still turned on too. I went to grab it out, but Dad stopped me. "Better wait until the doctors say to take that out, kiddo."

"Is it Christmas?"

"Day after." A tear fell from his eye. He blinked it away quick, but I caught it. "The doctor said you needed time to rest and get better."

"Get better? But I wasn't sick."

He stopped and looked away. "Theo, something happened at home. An accident."

"Like with a car?"

He shook his head. "No, not that kind of accident. There's something called carbon monoxide. Sometimes something goes wrong . . . and it's a gas . . . and you can't smell it like you can gas that goes in the car or that Mom uses to turn the stove on. So nobody knows when this gas is in your house. But if it gets into your house . . . it's poison."

"Poison?"

"It's really dangerous." He took my hand, but it slipped in his sweaty palms. "That's why they have an alarm to tell you when it's there. The alarm can sense the gas, and it will beep really loud if it's there so you know that you have to get out."

"Like a smoke alarm tells you that there's a fire?"

"Just like that." His lips shook like my hands would when I made a fist. "We have one . . . but it wasn't working." He swallowed hard and started crying harder. "I'm so sorry, Theo. I should've made sure. I should have been . . ."

"Where's Mom?"

He squeezed my hand tighter and then tensed his lips tight.

"I want to see Mom." I tried to get out of bed, but he eased me down and wiped a tear from my cheek. "I want to see Mom and Melanie," I said. "Where are they?"

"They went to heaven to be with Grandma and Grandpa."

"No, they're okay. I saw them." I shook my head. "They got Mom out of the house and brought her here with me, and they brought Melanie here in that bag so she wouldn't be cold."

"Theo, I'm so sorry," he said. "I know this is hard to understand."

"No, they have to be okay. We have to do Christmas. We have to go and open our presents and see what Santa brought us. I saw him, Dad. I saw Santa. He was outside with us. So I know he must've come. And we have to have Mom there so Melanie and I can open our presents. We have to show you the snow globes that Aunt Phyllis got us. We have to show you, Dad."

He pulled me into a tighter hug and pressed my head against his chest. "I'm not going anywhere, Theo. I promise you. And you're safe now. You're safe."

I cried harder into Dad's shirt until I fell asleep again and dreamed that Santa got me Pikachu. That we were all okay and safe. Why couldn't that dream be real?

We went home two days later. Dad said all the bad gas was gone now and our house was safe again. We weren't even home an hour when we changed into suits so we could go bury Mom and Melanie. The Church still had all the Christmas decorations up behind the coffins. I asked Dad if I could see Mom and Melanie, but he said that would upset me more. So we kept them closed. I just kept looking at a big picture of Mom holding Melanie we took a few weeks ago.

Dad and I stood in front of the coffins while crying people I didn't know well walked up and told us how sad they were. I couldn't stand there much longer, so Dad had me go sit down. Aunt Phyllis came in and walked right to me. "Hey, TJ. How are you doing?" It was the first time she ever said my name right. She

When Miracles Can Dream

hugged me and kissed my head. I tried not to cry. I didn't want her to think I was a baby.

The nice nun who works at our Church came in next. Sister Olivia Augusta, but we all just called her Sister Olivia. She walked to Dad and hugged him. Then to me. She kneeled down in front of me and hugged me too. "Oh TJ, I'm so sorry." She rubbed my curls like Mom used to. For a second, I tried to pretend like it was Mom doing it one more time.

I don't remember anything else about the funeral. Just that I wanted to kiss Mom and Melanie goodbye and tell them that I was sorry.

Dad took down the tree that day. It wasn't even New Year's yet. I wanted to keep it up a few more days. But I didn't want to fight with Dad either.

I found a wrapped box on my bed that night. It said, "To: TJ. From: Santa." I pulled the lid off, and it was Pikachu inside. Just like I'd asked him for.

I had asked Dad about Santa saving me. He said that the ambulance people told him that a neighbor had called 911 and gotten me out of the house. I don't remember a neighbor that looked like Santa, but Dad told me not to keep bringing it up. I figured he must've been right. If Santa really came that night, he would've gotten Mom and Melanie out too. Later, Dad told me he and Mom bought me Pikachu. Not Santa.

Francesco

If Santa didn't come that night to bring me Pikachu or to get me and Mom and Melanie out before the poison gas got us, he must've not been real.

We donated all of Mom's and Melanie's things to poor people at Church the next Christmas. I gave Pikachu too. Playing with him made me think of that night.

If I couldn't use him, I wanted to give him to a kid he wouldn't make sad. Pikachu deserved that.

Some days Aunt Phyllis would stop by the house and stay with me, but Dad didn't want to burden her. So I started working with him at the store after school. I would do my homework and then help put things out on the shelves. The store got really busy around Christmas time. We had all sorts of decorations there. But we didn't put any up at home the next year. Or the year after.

Even after four years, we still haven't put any up.

Not that we're home much to see them, so I guess it doesn't matter.

Aunt Phyllis doesn't have her party anymore. She had a stroke a few months after Mom died. She can still talk, but now she lives in a nursing home far away.

On Christmas Eve, Dad and I usually stay late at the store. I miss our old Christmas traditions, but I don't want to ask Dad to start them up again. If it doesn't make him mad, it makes him cry.

When *Miracles* Can *Dream*

But it's November now. And even with Christmas lights all over the store, it just doesn't feel like Christmas is coming.

I never wrote to Santa again. I even tried not to look at the Santa's Workshop section of our store. I tried not to even think about him. And it worked too.

Until today.

Because Santa just walked into our store.

Chapter 2
Micah

It breaks my heart seeing my son's face when Ed walks into the building. Ever since my wife and daughter died four years ago, Theo hasn't been the same. Although I suppose neither of us are.

Then again, he's still a kid. He was there when it happened and was the only survivor. I can't imagine how much harder this has been on him. Right after it happened, he kept talking about seeing Santa outside. I figured it was just the fact that it was Christmas Eve and he was still only six. The doctors wrote it off as just a coping mechanism. I thought he was finally past it.

Now I'm not so sure. There's almost a tear in his eye. He tucks himself behind the Christmas stocking rack, looking like he wants to run, but frozen in place.

"Thank you for seeing me, Mr. Trader." Ed extends a hand and recaptures my attention.

I shake his hand and fake a smile. "Pleasure's all mine, Mr. Gabriel." I lead him to my office in a corner of the store, sneaking one last glance at Theo.

I close the door to cut out the noise of the crowds and carols playing over the radio. I give Ed the once-over. Aside from being a little bit leaner than your standard Coca Cola Santa facsimile, it's astonishing how much he looks like "the real deal." No wonder Theo was captivated. Real white beard that isn't too long to attract attention. Glasses that almost disappear onto his face, just barely framing his gentle blue eyes.

"So I suppose I don't have to ask why you're applying to be our Santa Claus, Mr. Gabriel?" I look over his resume. "Seems you have a good deal of experience with it and obviously, you were blessed with more than a passing resemblance to 'Santa.'"

He chuckles and strokes his beard. "Well, one of my life philosophies is that if God blesses you with a gift, you should make every effort to put it to proper use."

"I guess my big question would be this." I point at him with my pen. "Given how you have the physical traits, how come you're settling for Trader's? You could probably get hired to do the same thing somewhere a little more prestigious? One of the high-end department stores. Maybe even the parade? Somewhere with much better pay."

He nods. "You're not wrong. I have been offered positions like that through the years. Even accepted a few of them from time to time." He folds his hands and leans back in his chair slightly. "I spent over thirty years in various 'office' jobs. I made a good living. Nothing that would get me a mansion with a big 'G' on the gates, but enough to retire comfortably. After so many years of routine work, I wanted to do something more rewarding. Those other places you mention are nice. The decorations are elegant, and the pay is good. But it all feels so corporate. One store didn't even let me speak to the kids. It was all about selling photography packages. Your store has a reputation of actually capturing the true spirit of the season and not just cashing in on it."

I flash to visions of my father greeting customers at the door, my mother handing out hot chocolate to the kids, or the both of them grabbing guitars and serenading people with carols.

"I guess I'll take the compliment." I click a pen and run through his resume again. "You're okay then with this being just for the holidays? Sales have struggled quite a bit the past few years, and payroll will be tight after the holidays are done."

He smiles and leans in closer. "I am perfectly aware of the terms of the position. This is my favorite time of year, but I'm not as young as I used to be. A job like this is the perfect way for me to engage the community while still remembering I'm well north of 70."

I smile and lean back into my chair. "Do you have a family, Mr. Gabriel?"

His smile vanishes a second, and he shakes his head. "I'm afraid it's just me."

"That's too bad. You seem like you'd be great with the kids."

He nods and lets out a deep sigh. "I suppose that's why I thank God for giving me a likeness to good ol' St. Nick. It helps to get me out of the house and feel like I am a part of someone's family for at least a little while. Maybe I don't have any grandkids. But one day, ten or twenty years from now, people will look back at the pictures of their little kid with 'Santa' and smile. So in some way, I get to still be a happy part of someone's story. Even if only a little part." He takes out a peppermint. "Do you mind? I know it's not quite professional, but my doctor does . . ."

I hold out my hand. "Say no more. My mom was diabetic. You're perfectly okay."

He pops it into his mouth and offers me one. I politely decline.

"What about you, if you don't mind my asking, Mr. Trader? Do you have a family?"

I nod to a picture of Theo on the desk. "My son, Theo. He helps out around the store. He's out there somewhere now. You'll be seeing him every day if you work here. He seemed to be quite taken with you."

Ed sighs. "Yeah, I noticed him staring. I take it he's still reeling from the loss of his mother?"

"How did you . . . ?" I knock a bead of sweat from my neck.

He points to the picture on my desk. "There's four of you in that family photo, but you only mentioned your son. Plus, I've studied enough kids to know grief, even the kind that's a few years buried."

"Carbon monoxide. A few years ago." I pick up the picture and remember the time we took it. Our last picture together. It rained so hard that day, and the kids' outfits were soaked. But somehow, the picture still turned out great. "It was Christmas Eve. Some sort of heater malfunction or something. When they were explaining it to me, I could barely pay attention. What difference did it make? It took my little girl and my wife . . . Christy was her name. Theo was in there too. By some miracle a neighbor got him out in time."

Ed gives me a strange look, almost as if he's familiar with the story. But he doesn't say anything and just reaches out and takes my hand. "It doesn't get easier, but you get stronger."

"So I've been told . . ." I think of the nights where I lay awake for hours, sobbing into my pillow so Theo won't hear me. The times I plastered over holes I punched in the wall when Theo was at school. The times I stood outside Theo's door as he wailed, wanting to go inside and hold him, but at such a loss for words I couldn't make myself take another step.

I spin my chair around so he doesn't see me cry. The last thing I need is to start tearing up in front of a job applicant. I take a deep breath and pretend to be looking through papers. I wait just long enough so my face is dry when I spin around. Perfect smile and dry eyes, an act I've become better at with each passing year. "I have nothing else. If you'd like to come and work for us for the next eight weeks, I'd love to have you."

He smiles and we shake hands. "Looks like we have a deal."

Francesco

"My father started this store more than forty years ago. He didn't have any big themes in mind. He just knew he loved all the seasons and he wanted to capture that in a store. Over the years, our reputation just kind of got away from us, and we were the talk of the town. Everyone from all over Cranivy Township would come to see our holiday light displays and shop our selection of floral displays, decorations, or the Christmas village. My dad was great with the customers. Mom too. I was always a lot more socially awkward. I usually felt a lot more at home in the back doing office work or unloading a truck. I didn't have the same decorative touch they did. My wife was great though. She was always able to plan the most elaborate displays."

"Well, the store is decorated really nicely now." Ed walks to a life-sized gingerbread house and steps inside to a life-size replica of a perfectly 1940s Christmas scene, complete with vintage toys under a tree adorned with old fashioned lights and ornaments. "I think somehow you figured out how to keep the standard up."

I shrug. "I can't quite take credit for all of that. I have a new manager here. Janny. She's the best. She can turn any mess of stuff into the most beautiful display you've ever seen. Christy was like that too. She actually worked here. It's how I met her. Dad saw her work at a local craft show and thought she'd be a great fit at the store. She was, too. Our displays got even more famous when she came aboard. I actually found myself enjoying being at work. I don't even remember when it happened, but at some point, I just realized I was in love with her. It wasn't long before we were engaged."

He smiles. "So she became your partner in this just like your mother helped your father."

I shook my head. "I thought it would be like that. I know Dad wanted us to be like that. But as soon as we had Theo, she resigned from the store to stay home with him. I couldn't fault her for it. As important as the store was, he was more important. But Dad passed away shortly after Theo was born, and then Mom developed pretty advanced dementia. By the end, she didn't even remember me. So that left just me to run the store. I had good assistants, but it wasn't until Janny came along that I really had someone else who could add that same magic Christy or my parents had."

"Well, hopefully I can help enhance that too," says Ed. He steps out of the gingerbread house twirling a plastic candy cane.

"Theo's actually really good too. He's got a lot of his mother's decorative touches." I spot Theo putting out our new additions to the Christmas village set.

One of them is Buddy and Jovi from Elf skating and we also have a replica of The Polar Express complete with Tom Hanks audio.

Ed belts out a laugh that sends a chill up my spine. For a split second, I almost forget that he's an actor. His voice sounds like every Santa laugh from every movie I grew up with. I suppose he's getting into character.

I call Theo over. I can see him hesitate, but eventually, he makes his way over. "Yeah, Dad?"

"Theo, this is Mr. Gabriel. He's going to be our Santa Claus this year."

He extends a reluctant arm and shakes Ed's hand. "Pleased to meet you, sir." He takes a step back.

Ed kneels down to eye level with him. "Hey, I hear things have been tough for you the past few years. I just want you to know that it's okay to feel sad. But remember that it's not your fault. And it is okay to enjoy Christmas again." He pats Theo on the head and for a second I see the faintest of smiles.

Ed turns to me. "I hope I didn't overstep. I know I'm still a stranger to you all."

"It's okay, Ed. Honestly, I think we all could do with the reminder." I turn to Theo. "Now, bud, I want you to help Mr. Gabriel here with anything he needs. You know how busy it can get around here at Christmas time, and I want to make sure Mr. Gabriel knows we have his back."

Theo nods and returns to the Christmas village, giving a few curious looks back along the way.

"He seems like a good kid." Ed and I begin to walk toward the floral department.

"He is," I say. "He's just been through a lot. More than a kid should have to go through. He used to smile all the time. Now, even four years later, it's still so hard to catch him with one."

"If it's not too forward of me to say, it seems like that may be true for the both of you."

"Well you got me there." I stare at the portrait of my father smiling over an archway. Even in that picture, his warmth and joy overflow and brighten the entire store. I wonder if there was ever a time Theo saw that look on me. "Christy used to say that about me even before . . . it happened. She always said she missed the smile she fell in love with." I tuck my hands in my pockets and stroll next to a line of pre-lit Christmas trees. "You know, I should've been home when it happened. The accident. My wife had asked me to come with them to her aunt's house that night. The store closed early for the holiday. I could have gone. But I stayed here late. A part of me wonders . . . if I had gone with them. If I had been home, maybe I could've gotten them out sooner."

"Or maybe you would've died too and Theo wouldn't have anybody. If I've learned one thing through the years, it's that you can't live your life running through what-ifs. You'll drive yourself mad, and over what? Something you can't control. That'll just be something else you regret when you're older."

We come to the garden area with illuminated Nativity figures and poinsettias lining a walkway into what remains of our harvest floral selection.

"Let me show you Santa's Workshop," I mutter through my pounding heart, hoping my attempt to change the subject works. We stroll to the other end of the section to a large indoor cottage adorned with hundreds of strings of colored lights. The walkway to it has seven different colors of candy canes. Figures of every conceivable North Pole character we can use without a licensing fee are popped all around the house. Elves and Mrs. Claus, nine different reindeer, and some odd depression-era children who I still think scare the kids.

Ed lets out another Santa laugh. "It's wonderful. I love it."

"You haven't even gone inside yet."

He claps my arm. "My friend, I have a good sense about these things."

I show him inside where everything is lit up only by the Christmas lights and even more of what's outside adorns the walls and walkways, leading up to a golden throne where he'd sit with the kids. I point to the camera positioned strategically. "We have this awesome nun, Sister Olivia, who comes every year to take pictures of the kids. She's a professional photographer. We have a special arrangement that half of the proceeds from the photographs go to the Church."

"That's extremely generous of you."

"Not as much as it sounds. Having someone do that kind of quality work without requiring payment up front is a life saver, and the traffic she brings into the store more than pays for it. Plus, I guess it's good to give to the Church this time of year. They took good care of us after it happened. Even if I'm not a regular there anymore, I still feel like I owe them everything."

"I don't think the Church is about collecting debts from people." Ed runs his hands down the arm of the chair. "But yes, I agree it's a very nice thing you're doing. Mr. Trader, I must say I can't wait to work with you. I think you'll find this will be the best year yet at the store."

I offer one of my signature half-smiles. A part of me hopes he's right. Another part of me is terrified at the thought.

Chapter 3
TJ

After just one day of having Mr. Gabriel as Santa, we had a line wrapped around the store. It wasn't even Thanksgiving yet. Now that he's been working here a few weeks, it seems like everyone wants to see him. Dad picked a good guy.

He looks like he should be playing Santa in a movie. His laugh is like Santa's. And his red suit isn't as faded as the Santa's at the mall. His has holly and cherries on his hat and golden lace all on the seams. And the red just seems deeper and brighter.

I watch as some of the kids sit on his lap and tell him what they want for Christmas. He doesn't do anything like in the movies where he starts speaking in foreign languages. It's more that when he talks to these kids, it's like he really knows their hearts. And they feel that.

Mr. Gabriel takes a dinner break at 5 o'clock. Dad has a small kitchen in the back with a fully stocked pantry and fridge. His dad started that tradition and says that taking care of the employees makes the store run smoother.

I follow him into the back and see him munching on half an Italian hoagie.

He sees me.

I duck behind the wall, as if he's dumb enough to think I just disappeared.

Francesco

"You can come in and sit."

I peek from behind. "I don't want to bother you if you're having dinner."

"It's always better to have dinner with someone else. Dining was meant to be a communal activity." He holds out a wrapped hoagie. "Plus, your dad ordered from Slack's. Best hoagie in the state."

"Yeah, I know, they're my favorite too." My stomach grumbles. I haven't eaten since lunch. I slowly inch toward him and sit in the corner at the other side of the table. "Thanks."

I take a bite and remember going there with Mom and Melanie the weekend before they died. Dad was with us too. He used to go out with us all the time when we were little. But, as we got older, he was away more and more. It was nice to have us all together again that night. I think it was probably the last thing we all did together as a family. We ordered our favorite hoagie from them. There are lots of good places to get a hoagie in our little town, but this one is the best by far. Our favorite had roast beef and turkey and provolone cheese and some weird blend of mayo and oil and vinegar that nobody else can make but the people at Slack's.

"You know, I know the guy who owns this place. He's a really awesome person. Gives a lot back to the community." Mr. Gabriel flashes me a smile. "How do you like yours?"

I nod. "It's good."

"Are you making up a nice Christmas list for your dad yet?"

I shrug. "I don't really want anything."

"A kid who doesn't have a Christmas list?" He takes a sip of ginger ale. "That would be a first."

"I help out here a lot. Don't really have much time to play." I remember the last time I played with Melanie. We dressed up as elves and pretended to be working on toys for all the kids in the world.

"You'll have the rest of your life to work. You won't be a kid much longer." He adjusts his glasses. "How about we combine the two? I can ask your dad if you can help me with the kids. We do need an elf to help at the line and to keep people engaged while they wait their turn. That can be you."

I shake my head. "I don't think so. Dad usually just likes me to stock shelves or sometimes set up some of the small displays."

He dusts the breadcrumbs from his hands. "Seems to me your dad just wants to keep an eye on you. As long as you're here, if you're doing something you enjoy, I doubt he'd object. Can't hurt to ask now, can it?"

I look away. Part of it sounds fun, but it would also probably make me sad.

"It might make you feel close to her again." He turns my head up.

My eyes burn, and I notice a tear in them. "What are you talking about?"

Francesco

"Your dad told me about your mom and your sister." He swallows hard and lets out a sigh. "I know what it's like to blame yourself for something bad happening, to feel like you shouldn't have been the one to get out safely. But blaming yourself doesn't make the hurt go away. Sometimes hiding from the things that make us think of them only makes us miss them more. I've found, if you miss somebody, the best way to feel close to them is to do something that reminds you of them."

I know he means well, but he wasn't there. He doesn't know what it's like to see your family die. He doesn't know what it's like to know your own dad hates you because you're the only one who didn't die.

He crumbles his trash into a ball and gets up from the table. "I do apologize. I barely know you and here I am trying to force you to do something. Whatever you do, it's something you should talk over with your father. Don't even worry about me and what I think." He tosses his trash and goes to leave.

"Wait!"

He turns around.

"I know this is a silly question, but the kids aren't back here." I take a breath and close my eyes and remember Santa's face when I opened my eyes. How his face looked like Mr. Gabriel's and how I know it was all a dream. "Do you think Santa's real? Like, the real Santa? I know you have to play him and convince kids that he's real and that you're him. But I'm not just a kid. I know my dad hired you, and I know you're not the real Santa Claus. But is there a real Santa?"

He walks back to his seat and looks me in the eye. "TJ, I believe Saint Nicholas was a real person who did many admirable things that eventually gave way to the legend of 'Santa Claus.' I think we all know a lot of the modern flourishes to the Santa Claus story are more to create a magical image for kids to cling to, to understand Santa. But just because some of these details may be fictional doesn't mean the entire concept of Santa Claus is as well."

"What do you mean?"

"Take me, for example. I play Santa Claus here at Trader's. To those kids, I am as real as can be. Just because I don't go into their houses and drop off their gifts doesn't mean I am a fraud. When I give them a candy cane, when I give them my time to listen to them and the things that are on their heart, I think that counts as giving something. I think when you give of yourself, that counts for something too. The real St. Nicholas did things for the good of others. When someone does good things like that, I think we can legitimately say that person is embodying the spirit of Santa Claus. Whether that's me, or Sister Olivia giving her time to photograph some really impatient kids. Or you, helping out your dad or doing something nice for a customer. When I do a good thing, I suppose you could say I'm Santa Claus at that moment. It doesn't have to be a joke or some meaningless nickname. And when you do a good thing, you can say you're Santa Claus. So, is Santa Claus real? I would say he is as real as the spirit of generosity in us. How real he is . . . that's up to us. Does that make any sense?"

I take out a picture of me and Melanie from my wallet that we took at the Amish Market a few weeks before she died. I was holding her on my lap and hugging her. I remember she cried on the way home. I don't remember why. Just that something upset her. Mom bought us funnel cake on the way out. I gave Melanie an extra piece, even though I wanted more. It made her happy and helped her stop crying. I wondered if that made me Santa like Mr. Gabriel said.

I press the picture against my chest and fight the tears burning my eyes.

"You were a good brother, TJ." He pats my shoulder. "And yes, that's exactly what I'm talking about."

I look up at him. How did he know what I was thinking?

He smiles. "Like I said, I know what it's like."

"I think that's a great idea." Dad smiles and claps me on the back. "It'll get you involved with the customers."

"I hope you don't mind. I suggested it to him before I came to you. Sometimes I get a bit ahead of myself." Mr. Gabriel approaches Dad. "If I overstepped, you just let me know."

When Miracles Can Dream

Dad shakes his head. "Absolutely not. I've been looking for a way to get Theo involved in something like this. I think this'll be a great opportunity." Dad turns to me. "Of course, that's if you really want to do this, Theo. Be honest with me. If it's too much, I'm not going to force you. I'd love for you to give it a try, but it's your decision."

I click my heels together. "Maybe I could try it." I look down a moment, but Dad turns my head up so he can see my eyes. "I loved when Mom and I decorated the house for Christmas, and I miss telling Melanie about Santa. I miss Christmas, Dad. I know you don't want to bring it home, but if I can do a little bit more here than just put things out or tell customers where to find something, maybe that would make it not so bad."

Dad's eyes tear up just a little and he ruffles my hair. "Then it's settled. You're gonna be Santa's elf."

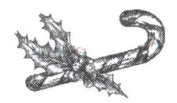

Mr. Gabriel has an elf costume ready for me within the hour. I go in the back and try it on. I'm surprised by how comfortable it is. I was expecting it to itch or pinch my nuts, but I actually feel better in it than I do in my regular clothes or pajamas. The hat is a lot smaller than Buddy's. Just a green felt hat with a little red stripe. The whole outfit is green with red trim and candy cane pins at the chest pocket and the sleeves.

Lucky there aren't any shoes so I can keep my

sneakers on. I don't think I'd like pointy shoes, and my sneakers are black anyway. So they should work.

I walk out to where my dad and Mr. Gabriel are waiting. "How do I look?"

Janny, my dad's manager, and Sister Olivia answer for them. Janny howls like Aunt Phyllis used to. "Oh my gosh, he is so adorable." She takes out her phone and snaps a few quick pictures.

"TJ, you make a very handsome elf." Sister Oliva circles me and gives me the once-over. "We should get you to Santa's throne and get some test pictures."

Dad folds his arms and lets out a chuckle. "You look good, Theo. The girls are gonna love you."

My ears get hot, and I take a step back. "You don't think I look dumb?"

Mr. Gabriel shakes his head. "From the guy who spends all day in a Santa suit, I think you look great. You need to be able to enjoy yourself and not worry about looking silly. That's the trick to owning this. If you think you look great, you'll make others agree."

I look in the mirror and see myself smiling. I do look kind of silly, I guess. But I also kind of like it. Maybe everyone else will too.

Mr. Gabriel comes over with the plastic candy canes we sell as lawn stakes. "This will complete the outfit."

I take the cane and twirl it in my hand like a real cane. I hear myself laugh. It's almost scary. I forgot what my own laugh sounded like. I hear Dad laugh, too, and it's good to hear that again.

I do a little dance around the cane. "Okay then, let's get some pictures."

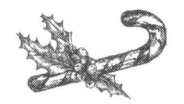

Sister Olivia moves so fast with her camera that I can barely see one flash before ten more pop up. "You're doing great, TJ. Perfect smile. Raise your head just a little. Perfect. Just a few more!" *Snap. Flash. Snap. Flash.*

She brings in Mr. Gabriel and has him sit in the chair with me on the side as the helper elf.

After only ten minutes, she has all the pictures she needs, and she brings us to her computer screen to look through all the shots. "These'll look great in the magazine advertisements we're going to take out for the store."

"Magazine advertisements? You think they're that good?" I raise an eyebrow.

She nods. "Definitely."

There must be over a hundred pictures on her screen. I never really like looking at myself in pictures, but Sister Olivia somehow makes me look okay in them.

"What do you think, Mr. Gabriel?"

He takes one of the printed pictures of the two of us. His smile goes away, and I see just a little bit of a tear come to his eye.

Francesco

"It's a great picture. People will love it." He puts it down again and tries smiling again.

He walks away and I follow after. "You okay, Mr. Gabriel?"

He motions with his hands for me not to worry. "Never better."

I hear him laughing again with the customers in a few minutes, but somehow it doesn't seem quite as full as it did before.

Chapter 4
TJ

Dad's friends at the printers can get anything printed just like that. It's only been two days, but they sent Dad a whole stack of pamphlets to advertise our store using my picture with Mr. Gabriel.

Dad and Sister Olivia decided to schedule a special Birthday Party for Baby Jesus for the first Saturday in December. We're going to get a doll and a big poster of Bethlehem and people will be able to take pictures with it. Sister Olivia says she can even get costumes for people to dress up in like shepherds and Mary and Joseph. Dad thinks people might still be scared of catching stuff like the flu. But Sister Olivia says she's seen it done in Boston and Miami and that people really liked it, so it's worth a shot.

Dad even got the local Knights of Columbus council to help sponsor it because Grandpa used to be a Knight before he died.

My big assignment today is to deliver pamphlets to all of the businesses on Center Avenue in downtown Cranivy. There are all sorts of places that would make good advertising.

I stop at Slack's and they let me leave a stack and post it on their Community Bulletin Board. So do Stoli's Steaks and Lucia's Italian restaurant. Even the Hong Kong Kitchen.

Francesco

I already left a bunch at school and Church. I left some at Kirk's Coffee House, but Vineyard Bar wouldn't let me come inside, so I didn't leave any there.

I come to a little street toward the edge of downtown called St. Joseph Street. I don't remember ever going down it before. It's between the bank and the daycare center. There's a lot of trees on it, unlike in the rest of town. I walk down it, and it leads to a lot of grass and a few religious statues. At the end of the road is a gate that's left slightly open, and behind it, there's a small church. It looks much older than St. Matthew's. But it's a lot smaller. Maybe only about as big as our house.

I wonder why Mom never brought me here. She liked everything about Church and made sure we went every week. Especially on holidays. Dad only goes to functions there now, not Mass. But he makes sure I still go to Mass every week because it's what Mom would want. And he made a promise to her at their wedding that he'd always make sure we went to Church if anything ever happened to her. Plus, the store has a lot of partnerships with the Church and the Knights of Columbus. Them seeing me at Church is supposed to help that or something. Still, I didn't know we had another church in town. I thought it was just St. Matthew's and Grace of Christ Baptist Church.

When Miracles Can Dream

I walk up to the door. It says something in Latin that I can't quite make out. Regina, something? C-O-E-L-I?

I push the doors open and walk inside. It's dimly lit, but I can still see lots of statues like at St. Matthew's. I hear men singing inside. As I listen closer, it sounds more like chanting. Their voices blend together and create almost an echo. I can't understand what they are saying, but their melody is beautiful and soothing. Like Mom's chicken soup.

I see an altar boy doing something with the candles on the altar. He looks like he's about my age. His hair is brown like Melanie's was, but thinner than mine.

As I walk closer, he looks my way and I freeze.

"Hey, welcome to Regina Coeli," he says. "I haven't seen you around here before. Do you need help finding something?"

I look around to make sure nobody else is listening. "Um, not quite. I was just leaving everyone in the neighborhood these little pamphlets for my dad's store. We're kind of having a birthday party for the baby Jesus in a few weeks, and we want to tell people."

"Really? That sounds awesome." He lights a candle on the altar. "Definitely leave some here. My mom would love that."

"You think you might come?"

He stops a minute and lights another candle. "Maybe."

Francesco

I look around at all the old paintings and statues on the walls. "I never saw this Church before. Nobody at St. Matthew's ever talks about it."

He laughs. "Well, it is kind of tucked away. You sort of need to be looking for it to find it. Or maybe sometimes you find it because you need to. Are you an altar server at St. Matthew's?"

I shake my head. "No. You gotta be in 6th grade to do it there. I'm only in 5th. Are you in 5th too?"

He gets quiet for a moment, but then nods. "We can start a little younger here."

"How come I've never seen you around? Like at school or anything?" I bunch some pamphlets into a perfect stack and set them down on a table by the door. "Are you homeschooled?"

He nods. "I guess you could say that."

"Do you like it?"

"I do. Do you like your school?"

I shrug. "It's alright. It's not bad. It's just . . . ever since my mom and my sister died, nobody really treats me the same." I think of all the friends I used to have in first grade. How they all seemed to be afraid of me after it happened. "Things like accidents don't usually happen in this town. So when they do, people kind of remember them, and it sort of becomes all they know about you."

"That sucks. You're a lot more than the bad things that have happened to you." He walks up to me and sits down in the pew in front of me. He motions for me to sit down, and I do. "Something bad happened to my family once, and it really kind of sucked. But the people who know me don't just see that. They see who I am. They see what I can give. They don't just see someone that something happened to. You know?"

I nod. "Yeah, it's not like that with me. My dad only sees what happened to my mom and my sister. And that I made it out. I know he loves me. But even four years later, that's still all he sees."

"Maybe we can help change his mind." He smiles. "I'll help in any way I can. You look like you could use a friend."

We fist bump. "Only if you get people to come to the Baby Jesus Party. My dad wants a big turnout for the store."

He motions for one of the pamphlets. "I'll talk to my mom about it."

I smile and give him a few. "Awesome. I hope I see you there." I get up to go. "By the way, I'm TJ."

"I'm Marcus. I'll see you around."

Chapter 5
Micah

I hired Janny Marto on New Year's Day last year. We had just packed away all of the Christmas clearance and gotten the Valentine's display up when a bus from the assisted living facility came in with fifteen elderly customers trying to get a head start for next year's shopping. Janny happened to be inside the store looking for an illuminated heart for the front window of her cottage when she saw what was going on. She stepped into action and took me aside with a decided "Show me the Christmas packaways."

I took her to our storeroom, half thinking she was going to lead the charge for discounted seasonal merchandise. Turns out she was doing crowd control. Within ten minutes, she had every single box emptied and sold to a mouthy octogenarian.

When the troupe of grannies was safely on their return shuttle, I took her aside. "Do you want a job?"

She turned to me and her auburn hair swayed like a breeze had just come in. "What makes you think I'd work for you if you don't already have the system in place to manage such a situation like we just saw?"

My mouth hung agape for just a moment before I threw on my best smile. "That's why I need a manager. I'm Micah Trader, the owner, proprietor, boss, or what have you. I've been running this store for a few years now and honestly, I need someone like you who can help me. I'm very good at office work, but I need someone who is quick on their feet on a sales floor. What you just demonstrated to me is exactly what I need in someone to manage my sales floor."

She pursed her lips, clearly trying to appear like she was debating it when she'd made up her mind. "That's awfully forward of you to confide all of those classified details about your management structure to a complete stranger. Not to mention you have no idea if I'm even in the market to work retail."

I scribbled down some numbers on my notepad, tore off a sheet, and placed it in her hand.

She took a look at it and her eyes doubled their size. "You're that desperate for me, just because I opened some boxes for some old ladies?" She crumpled the paper into a ball. "You could just outright ask me out instead of this song and dance with the job."

"Now who's making assumptions?" I leaned in close. "Like you said, I don't have the management structure in place to deal with situations. I'm a practical man, though. If I identify a problem, I like to rectify it as soon as I can. So what do you say? Will you come work for me?"

She flashed a grin. "I'll start tomorrow?"
"8AM."

Dad always wanted a Baby Jesus birthday party, but he never figured out how to get it off the ground.

When *Miracles* Can *Dream*

Tomorrow, I'm going to attempt to complete that dream for him. I've been running this store for years. It's been hard at times, but I think we're doing okay. With Janny's help this past year, we've definitely improved our standing. Between Ed and Theo's help, we've gotten the word out for this all over Cranivy and even into surrounding townships. I'm afraid to get my hopes up, but I think we're going to have a great turnout.

Janny brings the backdrop up with Sister Olivia to a closet we cleaned out in the back. It makes a perfect little portrait studio. The camera is all set up and Sister Olivia has already brought in enough costumes to fill several Nativity scenes.

I survey the area and flash a grin. "We're really doing this."

Sister Olivia takes a life-size plastic doll of a Baby Jesus and places it in the manger in the center of the makeshift stable.

She returns to her camera and takes a sample picture. "Oh, just beautiful. Perfect."

Ed claps me on the back. "I think this is going to be a rousing success."

I spot Theo toward the front door, sweeping up. I wave him to come over and see the set up.

He gives it a good look over. "It's nice," he says.

"Just nice? I think it's amazing."

He shrugs. "It's cool. I think people will like it."

Francesco

He inches back to the broom, head down as he sweeps the same spots he's already cleaned.

I follow on after him. "Theo, you don't have to sweep anymore. The floor's clean." I reach out and touch him, feeling a slight recoil as my hand rests on his shoulder. "Everyone got the store pretty recovered today."

"I'm just trying to keep busy," he says.

"Why don't you come and see everyone? There's no need for you to stand here all alone." I turn his head up and see that same lifeless look I see in the mirror every day. Not tears. Just empty. I hate seeing that in him, although I wonder what I can do about it. Since the accident, it just seems like we're both kind of aimless.

Ed comes over and puts his arms around the both of us. "How about the boss and his son get the first picture?"

"I don't think that's a good idea." I take a step away. "How about we just do Theo? There's no need for two guys in the picture anyway."

Theo looks over at me and I see his eye twitch like every word I said just stabbed him in the heart.

"Nonsense." Ed eases the both of us toward the area of our stockroom we partitioned off as a dressing room. "You can be St. Joseph, Mr. Trader. And TJ, you can be a drummer boy. It'll be perfect."

"A drummer boy? Ain't I a little big?" Theo tries to break free, but Ed coaxes both of us into the dressing room.

"You'll both look great. Plus, seeing the boss and his family in a picture will be good for promotion."

He closes the door behind us, and I'm left with Theo, a bunch of costumes, and a blaring silence.

I turn to Theo. He runs his hands through the clothes. "Well, I guess we should just make them happy. Right?"

I walk to a brown robe that looks like it's about my size. "I guess they won't leave us alone unless we do it. We don't have to keep the pictures or anything."

"Why couldn't we keep them, though?" Theo shoots me that empty stare again. "Until the other week, nobody took a picture of me since Mom did on Christmas Eve. Not one picture. Not on my birthday or Christmas. We don't celebrate anything anymore."

"Theo..." I rub my brow. "Now's not the time. You know we're always busy here. We have to work hard so everyone else can have a better holiday."

"We're closed on Christmas. And Easter. And Thanksgiving. We still don't celebrate it at home. If I'm lucky, we go out to dinner. Or you'll tell me to just order something from Amazon. But once we leave this store, it's like holidays don't even exist. We don't even have any pictures up at home anymore.

Francesco

Not even of Mom or Melanie. And then when I'm not as happy in front of people as you want me to be, you say you don't know why."

I ease myself into a seat. I really don't want to deal with this right now. Theo just doesn't understand how those things bring up that night. How I wasn't there. How I almost lost him. How we're better for keeping our eyes focused on practical things instead of getting caught up in sentiment. Because the sentiment just makes it hurt more when those things end.

"Look, if you want to keep a copy of this picture in your room or something, I'm not going to stop you, Theo. I've never told you that you couldn't have pictures in your room. Your room is your room." I turn his face to me. "But you don't have pictures in your room. Because deep down, you don't want to be reminded either."

He takes a step back. "Let's just take the pictures so they'll leave us alone." He takes one of the off-white robes and slips it on. Then he puts on a shepherd's cap and picks up the small plastic drum they have.

I put on the St. Joseph robe and we go out.

Sister Oliva and Mr. Gabriel fawn over us. I keep my smile posted best I can to avoid cringing.

"We do need a Mary for the picture, though," says Ed. He looks over and spots Janny straightening a sign promoting the party. He waves her over. "Janny, you would be perfect."

When Miracles Can Dream

She freezes and takes a step back. "I don't think Mr. Trader wants a third wheel in his picture."

"Mr. Trader doesn't want a picture at all. If we're just doing this for the sake of promotion, we might as well get a full picture. That sign will look much better if we have a visual to go with it. It'll only take a few minutes."

"I think Janny is probably wanting to get home, Ed," I say. "She doesn't want to pose for a promotional pic with the boss."

Ed already has her ushered into the dressing room.

Sister Olivia takes us to the stable. "I think having Janny play Mary in your picture is a great idea. It's a picture, Micah, not a date."

She brings Theo into the scene first to take some solo pictures. Theo looks like the saddest drummer boy ever. Not because he's crying or pouting. He'd probably look happier then. He just looks broken. And I know it's not something a Christmas tree or a picture on the wall can fix. Even if he thinks those things will somehow make what happened to his mom and sister hurt less.

Janny comes out dressed as Mary. And for a second my heart stops. I flash to Christy on our wedding day. How her white dress sparkled in the lights of the Church. How it felt like forever as she walked down the center aisle, inching closer and closer. Then I think of how radiant she looked when I saw them wheeling her out of the hospital with Theo in her arms. At that moment, I felt like nothing could go wrong. That I had my life figured out. I wondered when I lost that feeling, because I know it happened long before our furnace malfunctioned and poisoned my family.

I snap myself back to this moment. Staring at my floor manager. And for the first time, I notice how her auburn hair frames her face. The Blessed Mother's royal blue veil goes perfectly with her strong and determined sky blue eyes.

"Micah, you look like you're seeing an apparition."

"I think the phrase is 'seeing a ghost.'" I crack a grin.

She smacks me with her sleeve. "You're not much on parody, are you?"

"Parody, sarcasm, I like 'em both," I say with a wink.

I lead us into the stable and we kneel down on opposite sides of Theo.

"Okay, Sister. We're ready for our close ups."

Sister Olivia comes in and positions us just right so she can capture the best angles. I see Ed watching from outside, cracking a grin at every veil straightening or her snide quips about our posture.

Then for five or so minutes straight, she snaps pictures. I think I'll be seeing those flashes all night long. She had to have taken darn near a hundred pictures.

They all appear on her laptop screen within seconds and we go through them. I can't deny, even with Theo's stoic expression, this does make objectively good promotional material for the party. Somehow, I make a surprisingly convincing Joseph. He's usually stern and serious in Nativity artwork anyway. And having to deliver a baby in a freezing barn in December? Yeah, he probably looked even more irate during the real thing than I do.

Janny looks graceful, though. Her smile is just understated enough to not feel posed or overbearing. Very natural. Probably like Mary really looked on that night.

Sister Olivia selects the best shot and prints out a copy of our picture. "Everyone's going to love this. They won't be able to resist getting one of their own."

Theo comes out from the back already out of the drummer boy costume. Man, that was fast.

I go to the back with Janny so we can get the costumes back and then get home. It's going to be a long day tomorrow.

"Well, I guess they were right," I say. "Those pictures look good and will definitely help convince people to get some done tomorrow."

She lifts off the robe and puts it back on the hanger. "Agreed. They'll like it. Theo didn't seem to like it, though."

"Theo's got a lot of walls up because of what happened. He's coming around, though."

"Maybe Theo's not the only one with the walls."

I slide my robe off and hang it back up. "What do you mean?"

Francesco

"Look, Micah. I know this isn't my place. But I've known you for a good year now. We work close. And you're a great guy. It's very obvious that you love Theo. But everyone heard your fight tonight. And we see every day how he's longing for someone to hold him. For someone to let him cry. To let him feel again. To live. You spend so much time and energy trying to make this store as great as it can be. And that's admirable. It's an inspiration to the workers. But at what cost? You can't continue to coast by thinking that everything's just going to work out with you and Theo. At some point, he's either going to leave and go find someone who will make him feel alive again, or he'll shut down completely and you'll lose him that way. You're the nicest person I've ever met, Micah, who works so hard to make everyone's life great but that of his own family. For some reason, you think you and Theo don't deserve to be part of life. You two are alive. You deserve to be happy just like anyone else."

She pats me on the shoulder. "I'll see you tomorrow."

She walks out and leaves me alone in the back, with her words just hanging there. Judging me.

I shut off the lights and come up front. Sister Olivia and Ed wait by the door for me to lock up. Theo's up there too, coat already on, straightening the reindeer on a shelf by the registers.

We all go out as I lock up.

When *Miracles* Can *Dream*

Driving home, I look over at Theo. "Thank you for your help, again. I appreciate it."

He doesn't say anything. He just stares out the window at all the houses passing us by. Most of them framed in colored lights and trees with twinkling displays.

Chapter 6
TJ

By 9AM, we're ready for the Baby Jesus party to start. The store is fully stocked with everything Christmas for the rush of customers. Up front, I'm running the snack table with goldfish, animal crackers, and "bug juice." Sounds gross, but it's actually pretty good. It's just 7up mixed with fruit punch. Miss Janny showed me how to mix it for when we run out and need more.

Miss Janny has been really great getting the store ready for this whole thing. She's got the music set up for people at just the right volume so it's not too loud, but people can still hear it. She even showed up this morning with a whole bunch of balloons from the dollar store down the street. She must have like a hundred of them. Red and green. I helped her tie one to every other aisle in the store so the whole store looks even more like Christmas than it usually does.

We even ordered a full sheet red velvet cake to sing "Happy Birthday" to Baby Jesus this afternoon. Red because Jesus died for us.

We're always busy this time of year, but when I look out the door as Janny goes to unlock it, I see something I don't ever remember seeing in front of the store. A long line wrapping around the building. I guess those flyers I left around town actually worked.

Francesco

I take my place at the snack table. It's also going to be my job to give everyone their number so they can shop while they wait their turn to get their picture taken.

We get through the line pretty quick. Everyone comes in, gets their number, and the ones with kids take a cup of goldfish and a juice. The kids really seem to like the bug juice, especially when they learn what it's called.

After about an hour, Marcus comes in with a woman. She has the same brown hair and eyes. I can tell she's his mom before he even introduces us.

"Hey man," I say. "You came."

"Did you think I'd miss this?"

I shrug. "I dunno. I mean, it's not like you knew who I was. You could've just smiled and then thrown all of these flyers away as soon as I left."

He chuckles. "It sounded fun. Mom thought so too. Plus, I wanted to hang with you for a bit. Would that be okay?"

"Sure." I move the extra box of goldfish off the second chair so he can sit. I give his mother a number and hand him a cup of goldfish.

I take a cup myself and roll some onto my tongue.

"You're allowed to eat the merchandise?" He sets his cup down on a shelf.

"As long as I don't get too carried away."

"Did you get your picture taken?" Marcus picks up a book on Nativity scenes and flips through it.

"Yeah, they're up on the wall in the back where the pictures are taken. The nun taking the pictures wanted to use them as an example of how good the pictures look. I think that's a little silly. It's no better than anyone else's."

He laughs. "Well, she takes the pictures. She must know what a good one looks like."

"I guess." I hand a cup to a kid with a smile.

"Something else bugging you?" He takes a sip of juice.

I lean into the table. "It's nothing. Just my dad. We kind of had a fight about Christmas and stuff. He's so into this store and making Christmas so magical for everyone, but at home, it's like he wants to pretend it doesn't exist. Sometimes I feel like he wants to pretend I don't exist."

"Just because your dad is really busy doesn't mean he doesn't love you."

I look over and see my dad helping at the photo booth in the back. I try to think of a time I saw him that happy at home. He always seemed happy in the store, but he never seemed to want to bring that happiness home. It's like he was happier here.

Marcus looks over at him. "Running a store takes a lot of work. I don't think it's you."

"It's not that he's busy. I know he works hard here. Sometimes it just seems like he doesn't even want to have time to be at home. Like, even if he doesn't have to work, he just hates being around me."

Marcus looks at me. "You should tell him how you feel. Maybe that will help him talk to you."

"What's *your* dad like?" I study his face to see if he reacts. He doesn't. Just a little twitch of his eye. "Your mom seems nice. But you haven't said anything about your dad."

Marcus looks over at my dad. He's with Mr. Gabriel, trying to get a little kid to smile for his picture by making funny faces. Marcus sighs. "My dad's great. He works a lot."

"So kind of like my dad?" I raise an eyebrow.

Marcus stares ahead. For the first time ever, I see his smile go away just a little. "A little. But I know that he loves me. And I know he works hard to make others happy. He tries the best he can to make me happy too."

I wipe a tear and lean back and think about all the things I used to do with Mom. All the picnics we'd do or trips to the store. Dad wasn't there for most of them. "At least you know your dad loves you." I see how Dad is with this stranger's kid. I wonder if he was ever that way with me. "I think my dad just takes care of me because he has to."

"Talk to him, TJ. He's your dad. The only one you've got. You can't keep going just thinking he hates you."

I want to believe Marcus. I want to think all I have to do is talk to Dad and everything's gonna be okay.

When Miracles Can Dream

But he doesn't know Dad. He knows his dad loves him. Things are different for me.

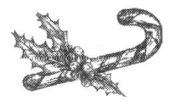

I can't believe my eyes. Aunt Phyllis walks through the front door of our store. She sees me right away. "How's my KJ doing?"

I run from my table to her and nearly knock her walker down.

Standing behind Aunt Phyllis, a Black woman dressed in a rose skirt stabilizes her. "Careful now. I know you think you're at 100% again, but you still have to be careful."

Aunt Phyllis brushes her aside. "Hogwash. EJ, this is Ally. She's my nurse. She thinks that means she knows what's best for me."

"You had a stroke," Ally says.

"I survived a stroke." She pushes us away from Ally.

"Are you feeling better, Aunt Phyllis?"

She laughs. "I feel sixty again. Can't complain."

I laugh. I remember how much Aunt Phyllis used to make Mom laugh. I didn't think I'd ever see her again after Mom died. She stopped by the house a few times and then Dad told her to stop coming. I don't think they ever got along. Then I heard she'd had a stroke. I wanted to visit her, but I was too scared to ask Dad. So we never did.

"How come you're here? Are you just here to see me or did you hear about the party?"

She laughs. "Someone posted some flyers on the bulletin board in the lobby, and I saw my favorite great nephew on it. Dressed in some goofy outfit, but still. Looked like fun. I figured it's been a while. Why not go see him? We always used to see each other every Christmas." She hugs me. "I've missed that."

"Me too." She seems unsteady unless she's holding the walker, but she's talking very well. They must be taking good care of her.

She looks over my face. "I know it's a cliché to say, but you remind me a lot of your mother. Especially when she was your age." She sighs and I see a tear come to her eye. "It's a real shame what happened. And that we were falling out of touch."

Ally leans in to her. "Mrs. Callahan, you should find a seat. You shouldn't be on your feet too long."

Aunt Phyllis rolls her eyes. "How about we get me one of those pictures with the baby Jesus?"

I raise an eyebrow. "You actually want to do that?"

"Of course. And I want you in the picture too."

"I . . ." I look at my table. "I have to watch this table. It's my job."

"You're not even eleven. Don't they have labor laws or something?"

"It's my dad's store."

"And? You can't get someone to watch it for ten minutes?"

I look around. I can't find Marcus anywhere. He must've been called to get his picture taken.

When Miracles Can Dream

I see Miss Janny and call her over and explain things. She agrees to watch the table so I can get a picture with Aunt Phyllis.

I hand Aunt Phyllis a number. "We're pretty busy. I think it's going to be a while before we're called."

"Then I guess I'll visit with you. That'll make the time go pretty quick."

I smile and nod and pull up a chair for her. I tell Ally she can look around and take a break while I sit with Aunt Phyllis.

"You know, your father didn't used to be like that." Aunt Phyllis sips a cup of punch. "When he and your mother first met, they were all bubbly and in love. She couldn't wait to bring him around to meet the family and he seemed to love being there."

She takes out a picture of them when they were still dating. I never saw it before. They're so young and almost don't even look like Mom and Dad.

"Wow, they look happy," I say. "I wish I could've seen Dad that happy before."

She sighs as she takes the picture and puts it away. "Your father isn't a bad man, but he's always been bad at confronting how he feels. I think he wanted to go to college and take up something. Business, law, I never really could get him to talk about it. But when his father's health took a turn unexpectedly, he had to not only step up to help at the store. He had to pretty much keep it afloat. It was either he run it or watch his father's life's work fall apart. Very George Bailey-like. Although praised be Jesus, your father didn't have an Old Man Potter to worry about. At least not beyond the standard struggles of running your own store. From what your mom told me, I get the feeling that it really took a lot out of your father."

"Why didn't he just ask for help?"

"Pride, stubbornness, maybe he didn't think anyone could. Maybe he did and it just wasn't enough. I don't know. All I know is, she felt him growing more and more distant as the years went by. Even though he was good at it and the store was doing well, he just could never seem to come home, even after the store was closed. I think sometimes she thought he was at the bar, but he never came home drunk. So she never knew for sure."

I look up at Dad at the picture stable. "I just wish there were more times I could remember when we were all together. So many of my memories, it was either just Mom and Melanie at home or me helping him here. I remember him playing with Melanie on the swings at the playground. And I remember them sharing a funnel cake at the mall. But I don't remember all of us doing things together. Am I crazy?"

She smiles and pats me on the head. "I think you're just growing up. As we get older, sometimes we forget the good times. Or at least the quiet good times, the typical day where nothing big happened. Sometimes

When Miracles Can Dream

those are the days we're the happiest. But we don't realize it, and so we don't think about remembering them."

"Number 57, you can come back to get your picture taken," Dad says over the speaker.

"That's us." I wave down Miss Janny, and she watches the table while I help Aunt Phyllis to the back.

"Phyllis!" Dad's eyes widen as he sees us coming back. "You're here? You look . . . well. How are you?"

She pushes past him. "You don't have to pretend to be happy to see me. I just want to get a picture with AJ and maybe get some of that cake he tells me you're gonna serve."

"Phyllis, you know I adore you."

"Haven't seen you in almost four years."

Dad freezes and his lips shake a little. "Things are complicated. I admit that. But I was still not happy to hear of your stroke. And I am legitimately happy to see you doing so well."

"My sentiments exactly." She cracks a grin. She has Sister Olivia get her a chair to sit behind Baby Jesus. Then she waves me to come kneel next to her.

"Shouldn't we dress up first?"

"Hogwash," she swats her hand. "We're getting our pictures as you and me. No need to dress up as somebody we're not."

Sister Oliva calls our attention to the camera. "Alright you two. Look right here at the smiley face." *Snap. Flash. Snap. Flash.* Before I even realize it, we have a bunch of pictures taken. Sister Olivia shows us to the printer screen.

I don't think I've ever had a picture with Aunt Phyllis before. These ones look good. Her smile is soft and she looks really happy. Even I look pretty happy in the pictures. It's good to have pictures of me and family again.

Aunt Phyllis buys two copies of each picture, one for her and one for me. They print them out and in a minute they are dry and ready. They email me copies too.

"Something to start up your photo album again." She smiles and pushes her walker back toward the front where Ally is waiting for her.

"Look at these. Aren't they beautiful?" Aunt Phyllis shows the pictures to Ally with a big smile.

Ally returns the smile and nods. "Yes, Miss Phyllis. They are lovely."

I spot Marcus and his mom looking at some of our Christmas statues. I run over and show him one of the pics. "Hey, check this out."

He chuckles. "That's cool man. Your aunt's awesome for taking a picture like that."

"Can I see yours?"

He shows me one of him and his mom dressed as angels. They're pretending to be singing like the angels in the Bible. "What do you think? Too goofy?"

I laugh. "No, it's fun. You should put it on your Christmas cards."

When Miracles Can Dream

Marcus's mom comes over and looks at our pictures. "Your picture looks great, TJ. You and your aunt are so cute."

"Thanks. You want to meet her?"

"Sorry, Marcus and I gotta go. Christmas stuff to do."

I sigh. "We're just about to cut the cake, though."

Marcus fist bumps me and smiles. "That's okay. More for everyone else that way. Stop by Church later; maybe we can talk after Mass."

"Yeah, I guess. Thanks for coming," I say. I wave to them as they leave, wondering if Marcus can talk to his parents better than I can talk to Dad. There goes having a friend to help me man the snack table.

At 3 o'clock, Janny sends me to the back to get the cake. Mr. Gabriel comes with me and helps me put the candles on it. Red velvet makes it the perfect color for Christmas.

"Are you having a good time, TJ?" Mr. Gabriel smiles at me as he puts in candles around the letters "Happy Birthday, Jesus."

I nod. "Yeah, it's good. People seem to be having fun. And a lot of people are buying stuff, which should make Dad happy."

"I saw you and your aunt getting your pictures taken. I snuck a peak at them while they were printing. I think they turned out well."

I nod. "Yeah."

Mr. Gabriel turns my chin up. "You know, TJ, I'm sure your dad would like to bring this out with you. Sort of make it a family thing, father and son. Why don't we go ask him?"

I roll my eyes. "Mr. Gabriel, you know my dad isn't going to want to do anything with me. Don't even waste his time."

He fixes his glasses on his face and nods. "Whatever you say."

Mr. Gabriel takes a lighter out of a drawer in the kitchen and lights all of the candles on the cake. One by one the striped candles start glowing, their red and green wax mixing with the white to make them look like candy canes.

He picks it up off the table and gently hands it to me. "Sure you can handle this by yourself, TJ?"

"Yes, I can do it." I tighten my arms around it and go back to the sales floor.

Janny has everyone gathered together. Just waiting for me.

As we walk out, everyone starts singing "Happy Birthday" the moment they see us. We put the cake down on a table and sing another verse. Sister Olivia and Janny get the little kids up front to start clapping along. Then I get to blow the candles out for Jesus. I wonder if I get to make a wish even though it's not my cake. Maybe since it's for Jesus, it's a prayer. I say it in my head anyway and hope maybe it could come true.

When Miracles Can Dream

The smell of candle smoke fills the area as Janny cuts little pieces for everyone and puts them on special Christmas plates with holly and snowflakes.

The kids all smile and give polite "Thank-yous" with each piece. I take one after everyone else has already had one, just to be fair. I take a bite and it's a really good cake. Not too sweet but still squishy and good.

I look over and see Aunt Phyllis having some. Her nurse Ally even has one.

Dad comes out from the back and tells everyone he hopes they're enjoying the cake.

He looks to Aunt Phyllis and then he freezes. I've never seen his face look so white and frozen.

"Ally?"

Ally looks up and sees my dad. "Hi, Micah."

What does she mean? We've never met her before. Why does it look like she knows Dad?

Chapter 7
Micah

I met Ally Carper the day my father started chemo. He'd been diagnosed with lung cancer a few weeks prior. Forty years of smoking out back by the delivery door finally caught up with him. He was a determined guy, though. Fought that cancer for four years before it finally won the fight. His Knights council gave a beautiful showing at his funeral. Everyone knew he'd lived and died with dignity, a bastion of strength and honor.

Still, from the time he started treatment, he would never be able to hold the same role at the store. It was a demanding job that he just didn't have the physical stamina to do anymore. So as he stepped back from primary duties, I had to step up.

Ally was in nursing school, just looking for an evening job to help with tuition and rent. I don't even remember the interview. Nothing of note happened. If she could run a cash register accurately and honestly, then the job was hers.

Christy and I had already been married three years by this point. I remember when we were newlyweds and we'd sneak to the back room to make out, or how we'd have hot chocolate dates in her lighted Christmas trail outside.

Sometimes when Mom or Dad was covering my shift, I'd sneak her off to dinner at Lucia's. Best

Italian restaurant in Cranivy. Heck, the best Italian restaurant in the entire county. The veal they served was so huge that it literally hung off the plate. They brought take-home containers to the table along with the food since nobody ever finished their portion in one sitting. Especially with their nationally famous French onion soup on the menu. I don't quite know how they get their cheese to bake so perfectly or how their broth manages to pack so much flavor without being a salty mess. But they pull it off.

One time I took her to this little village of stores with a colonial theme that sold everything from flavored honey to licensed throw pillows. Honestly, every store we went into gave me ten new ideas for sprucing up my store. Life was good for us as newlyweds. Until it wasn't.

One of the things we'd always looked forward to was children. Having a bunch of kids running around the house or reading to them stories I remember my dad telling me as a kid, it was a dream. It was all we talked about. And we kept waiting for the day we'd finally get word that we were expecting. Sometimes we'd buy a random test in the dollar store just to see if maybe we were pregnant and Christy just didn't have symptoms yet. Those tests always came back negative.

After two years of no luck, the strain began to wear on us. I don't know why. We knew couples who waited much longer. Maybe it was the stress of my increased workload at the store coupled with the frustration of parenthood always slipping away. Where our time together was once fueled by romance, now it was just so empty. I'd come home late, dead tired and half asleep. Any romance was just to try for a baby. And even that became more and more rare as we approached our fourth Christmas together.

It was Christmas Eve. We'd just closed up the store for the evening at 4PM. Christy had gone over to her aunt's house. Dad was having a treatment week and so Mom and Dad went to a relative's house to take it easy for the holiday.

I knew what awaited me at home. Christy had already decorated the house brighter than most of the areas in the store. She'd probably have a late supper ready, complete with wine and chocolate truffles. She'd try to put some romance back into our love life and make it not such a chore anymore. And I just didn't want to deal with it. Maybe God just didn't want me to be a father. Maybe this store was all I'd get.

Ally and I were closing out the day's funds in the office when we got to talking. She had just gotten out of an abusive relationship a few months before she moved to Cranivy. She was hoping to work in geriatrics to honor her late grandmother who practically raised her. She was dealing with bouts of depression and anxiety. She wasn't looking forward to going home to spend the holiday alone either.

Francesco

I don't even know how it began. It was all such a blur, like a dream you only remember flashes of. I must've known enough to lock up.

I remember opening my eyes. We were at her apartment. I remember thinking how drab it was compared to my home. It was barely even a studio apartment. Only had a single window to the outside with a tiny Christmas tree that looked like it was thrown together with five bucks' worth of stuff from the dollar store.

I could feel her skin against mine. My heart pounded my chest and my mind screamed at me. *Christy.* You just betrayed the best woman in the world, stupid. On her favorite holiday no less.

I remember Ally getting up and throwing on clothes. "I'm sorry. This shouldn't have . . . I'll hand in my resignation after Christmas."

"Ally . . . You don't have to."

She held out her hand. "No, Micah. I do have to. I can't stay there. Not after this. It wouldn't be right and it would be unfair to all of us."

I laid my head back and considered how I could look my wife in the eyes and tell her that I'd just broken our vows. Should I even tell her? Would it do any good to break her heart if this was never going to happen again?

I must've gotten dressed and left because the next thing I remember is pulling in the driveway, a gas station bouquet of roses on the passenger's seat.

When I walked through the door, I saw her sitting on the couch, sipping from an "I'm Only A Morning Person After Coffee" mug.

"Hey, hon," she said. A gentle smile slowly made its way onto her face. "Home pretty late, huh?"

"Yeah . . ." I handed her the roses. "A lot of last-minute bookkeeping things at the store. I'm sorry. I know you wanted me to go with you to your aunt's. Maybe tomorrow we can do something."

"Micah, it's okay." She patted the seat next to her on the couch, and I sat down.

"Merry Christmas, honey." I leaned in and kissed her, my insides tearing at me as I thought of waking up in someone else's bed.

"I have a Christmas present for you. And I can't wait until morning to give it to you." She took out a pregnancy test and handed it to me. It read "positive."

I stared at it in disbelief, every thought of parenthood and betraying her swirling in my head like a storm. "You're sure?"

She nodded, crying and smiling all at the same time. "I am. I can feel it. I'll check with my doctor this week, of course. But this is it, Micah. This is what we've been waiting for." She held her stomach and rubbed it gently. "We're finally going to have the family we always wanted."

I placed my hand on her stomach and imagined the life we'd dreamed of. And I wondered how it could possibly exist with the dark cloud I'd just made hanging over us.

I threw my arms around her and hugged her. "This is the best Christmas gift we could ever get."

Tears burned my eyes. She thought they were happy tears, like hers were. And some of them were happy. And some of them were because, in that moment, I hated myself.

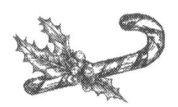

When I returned to work on the 26th, they told me Ally had resigned. When I returned to her apartment so I could apologize, she'd already moved out. A part of me was relieved. Maybe, just maybe, if she wasn't there to remind me, I could forget about what happened and focus on being a dad to my child.

I found romance returning to my marriage. I would come home excited with a new baby toy. I brought home catalogs with nursery furniture so we could pick through them together. At about seven months, we both gave in and decided to find out the gender. We were having a little boy. The son I'd dreamed about having since I was a boy myself.

It was July when the day came. Christy's water broke and we drove her to the hospital. Everything moved so fast. The doctors said a lot of things that I barely remember. All I know is I had to stay in the waiting room while they wheeled her in for an emergency c-section.

When Miracles Can Dream

It wasn't even an hour yet when I saw them wheeling in Ally. She was screaming and crying. "It's too soon. I'm only 28 weeks."

I ran to her and took her hand. "Ally?"

She looked up at me with tears. And somehow, I knew. Before I even looked down and saw her stomach, I knew. She was pregnant. And it was mine.

They wheeled her into delivery, and I stood there with my guts hanging.

The doctor came a short while later and told me that our son was here. They put me in all the right gear and brought me in to see them.

I saw him in Christy's arms. Theo, my little boy. In that moment, I didn't think I could love something so much. His eyes were already open, looking around, taking in the world. But he was quiet. He wasn't crying or fussy. Almost like he was already contemplating something. And his hair. He already had a full head of auburn hair.

"This is our son," Christy said. She handed him to me.

I sat down next to her and stared into the face of love itself. "Hey, Theo. It's me. It's your dad." I didn't know what else to say. What could I say? After what I'd done, and now, just a few rooms away, it was about to become something I could never get over.

Francesco

Theo and Christy were asleep within an hour. So I went to check on Ally. The delivery had gone well, but the baby had to be kept in the NICU. She gave birth to a girl. A beautiful baby girl. They said she had Down Syndrome. But that didn't make her any less beautiful. I remember standing above her incubator, thinking how beautiful she was. How I could already love someone so much, even knowing how much trouble could be awaiting because of how she was conceived. But for one night, I put all of that out of my mind and just took in these new humans who I already loved so much.

Ally named our little girl Kelsey. Theo was able to go home after three days. Kelsey had to stay over two months before she was able to go home.

Ally agreed to keep Kelsey's existence a secret from Christy. She didn't need to be burdened with that now. She had a newborn to take care of. For my part, I sent Ally money every month. I even visited Kelsey often. I told my family I had to work late, but most of those times, I was with Kelsey. She had challenges, but with Ally's guidance, she was able to show everyone how smart she was.

Somehow, I convinced myself I could keep these two lives separate forever. I should've known eventually, they'd crash.

Chapter 8
Micah

I call Ally to the stockroom, away from the crowds and Theo.

"Ally, it's good to see you. But why are you here?" I fold my arms and lean against a shelving unit full of Nativity scenes.

"Wow, Micah. That's quite a range of feelings in just a few words."

"I thought we agreed you wouldn't come to the store."

She rubs her brow and shakes her head. "Micah, we also agreed you'd be an active part of Kelsey's life. You haven't been to see her for months."

"I know. I've been meaning to get back."

"You used to come all the time. Ever since the accident, it's like you're trying to erase her."

I take her into the kitchen and ease her into a seat. "It's complicated. I have Theo to consider. It's not easy to just take off like it was when Christy was alive."

"That is such bull, Micah. I think you blame Kelsey for what happened because you were with her."

"No." I shake my head. "I don't blame anyone. It was an accident."

That's a lie. I blame myself. I've spent so many years trying to hide Kelsey and yet not abandon her or Theo, that I think I've abandoned both of them.

Francesco

"Look, Micah, I'm not even here for you. Phyllis is a resident at the home I work for. When they assigned her to me, I didn't even know she was related to you. I didn't figure that out until much later, and by that point, I'd come to care for her. And she wouldn't have anyone else be her nurse. She wanted to come to this today. Because you used to be family. I figured it would be more suspicious if I tried too hard to talk her out of it. I tried not to call attention to myself. Which was going fairly well until you called me back here in front of everyone. Your son's not going to wonder about that at all."

She's right. I messed up. I get up and begin to pace, trying to figure out how to make all of this mess right again. How could anything be right again? I betrayed my family, and now another person was involved and would be forever.

"I'm sorry, Ally. I know this isn't your fault."

She gets up and looks me in the eyes. "I know it's not as easy as it sounds, but why don't you just tell people about Kelsey? About what happened? They'll be mad, but maybe they'll forgive you. You think this has been a cake walk for me? You don't think I'd have liked to have had a child with someone who wasn't married? Who didn't have a family of his own already? But I made a choice. I own what I did, and I do my best every day to give my daughter the best life I can. I'm not just trying to throw enough money at her to ease my conscience."

When Miracles Can Dream

Her words sting my chest. "That's not fair."

She shakes her head. "Yeah, well neither is having an absentee father because he cares more about what his 'real' family thinks of him than he does about your happiness. You know what the irony is? From what I can tell, you're so busy trying to keep this secret, you've managed to neglect both your son from your wife and the daughter from the affair you'd like to forget."

"What do you mean?" That voice. My heart stops. No.

Ally and I freeze.

We both look over at the same time to the doorway. Theo.

His eyes fill with tears and he takes a step back. We were talking so loudly. I got so caught up in the moment, I didn't even think about someone coming in.

"Theo, let's come in here and talk."

"No. Get away from me." He curls his lips into a pout and tries to fight the sobs.

I take a step toward him. "I don't know how much you heard, but we should talk about it."

"Talk about it? Talk about what? You never want to talk about anything. Guess now I know why."

He turns to run away.

I dash after him.

"Micah, I'm sorry." Ally follows after. Her cell phone goes off and she answers it.

Francesco

Theo runs past Sister Olivia and Ed to the door. He's already grabbed his coat and thrown it on.

"Theo, wait. I know you're upset, but you need to let me explain."

He turns around. "Just because I'm still a kid doesn't mean I don't understand what you did. You can't explain away what you did to Mom. Go be with your other family and leave me alone. It's what you do best anyway."

Then he's gone out the front door.

"Theo!" I follow him outside and look in all directions. He's gone. How did he get away so freaking fast?

Ed runs up to me. "Micah, what happened?"

My eyes burn, and I try to talk, but the words don't come out.

He places his hands on my shoulders. "Focus. What happened?"

"He overheard something. Ed, we've gotta find him. He's upset. What if he hurts himself?"

"We'll find him. Don't worry. Then we'll all sit down and sort this out."

Ally screams. She runs up front. "Micah!" Her eyes stream with tears.

"What's wrong?"

"It's Kelsey."

My heart hits my stomach again. "What about her?"

"Her caretaker just called. She got out of her room and . . . I don't know what happened."

"What do you mean happened? Where is she?"

"She fell down the stairs, and they took her to the hospital. They don't know how she is."

Everything starts spinning. I don't know where Theo is, and now Kelsey is in the hospital hurt. The crowds in the store are bigger than ever. They all watch us with judging eyes.

Ed takes me aside. "Micah! I need you to pull it together. We're not going to do either of them any good by panicking."

Ally rustles through her purse for her keys. "I need to get to the hospital. You all can do what you want." Everything in her purse hits the ground. She falls to her knees and tries to cram it back inside.

"You can't drive like this." I kneel down next to her and help her gather it all up.

"Well I'm not staying here."

Ed claps me on the back. "I got Theo. You take her to the hospital and sort all of that out."

"I can't leave him right now."

Ed pushes me toward the car. "Right now, I think seeing you would just upset him more. He couldn't have gotten far. Let me get him." He calls over to Janny and Sister Olivia. "You have things here?"

"Sure thing." Janny comes to us and helps Ally to her feet. "You all go."

Francesco

Phyllis comes out and looks at the situation. "What's going on here? I saw CJ running out crying. What did you say to him?"

Ally looks to her, then to her car. "I have to get her back. I can't just leave her here. They could fire me."

"Back? I ain't going anywhere until my nephew's back safe."

Janny takes Phyllis aside. "You can stay here with me. You can maybe help get the kids to smile for the pictures."

Phyllis protests, but Janny has her inside in a few seconds anyway.

"Call your work." Ed helps her to her car. "Explain the situation. They'll send someone to get her. Micah, you stay with her. I'll find TJ. I'll make sure he's safe."

I freeze for a minute. The world stops and instead of spinning, now everything is frozen. I think about Kelsey. She is nothing but love and smiles. Knowing she's hurt crushes everything inside of me. And Theo. I've spent his entire life walking on eggshells to avoid looking him in the eye, knowing I betrayed his mother on the night we found out he was coming. And because of that, he's grown up sad and resentful. And now I may have just burnt the last bit of trust he has in me. Our town is small and safe, but anyone running away while that upset isn't thinking clearly. What if he hurts himself, or worse?

"Micah. I know you haven't known me that long, but I've come to care about you and Theo like family," Ed says. "I need you to trust me."

I look into Ed's eyes. He has the gentleness and strength I remember in my own dad's eyes. Like when I woke up in the hospital and he was there, telling me that everything would be okay.

I nod and brush aside a tear. "Call me as soon as you find him."

"I promise."

I take Ally to my car and we drive off for the hospital. As I see the store disappear into the distance, my mind screams to me that everything left in my life that I love is disappearing further and further into the rearview.

Chapter 9
TJ

Those words swirl in my head as I run away from Dad's store and into our town. All around I see everyone going about their Christmas planning. Shopping or stopping for dinner. Kids spending time with their mom and dad who love them and want to spend time with them.

Dad had a kid with someone else? He cheated on Mom? And he kept all of it a secret? When? Was that why he was never home? Did he like being with them more than us? I want to go back and yell at him and tell him how I feel, but I also don't want to see him. Because just thinking about him makes me think of Mom. Did she know? I remember that last night, she kept looking at the door. Like she saw him coming or was hoping he'd come in. She just wanted him to be there with us, and he couldn't even give us that. Maybe he could've gotten them out in time.

I walk down a street, hands in my pockets because it's starting to get really cold. The sun's setting really early now so all of the Christmas lights are on. Every single store has its front window lit up in all sorts of Christmas colors. The restaurants all have a big tree and decorations to get people to come inside.

In the town square, there's a big fountain that they had turned into a big Christmas wonderland. They put up a tree like twenty feet tall with a huge star on top and gold trimming and more lights. They have a light-up reindeer and snowman, and a big Santa that looks a little bit like Mr. Gabriel too. Walking through it, some of the light-up figures are taller than me. They have characters from movies that move and wave. One time, I wave back. What if they were real? If I could go with someone like that and have an adventure with friends who cared about me. Friends who actually wanted to hang out with me. Not like in real life where everyone's nice enough to wave and say "Hi," ask me to help them find something, then wish me a Merry Christmas. But then I go home and I'm alone. Even Dad doesn't want me to bother him or do anything to make him think about Mom.

I wonder if Dad is looking for me or if he cares more about finishing the party first. It's probably about to wrap up by now. Once everyone is out and they count all the money, he'll probably send Janny or Mr. Gabriel to try and bring me home.

As I keep going, I hear the chants from that Regina Church breaking into the Christmas carols coming from the stores. *"Veni, Veni Emmanuel."* The singing is deep and slow but kinda relaxing. I turn and go toward the Church. Maybe Marcus is there and he can cheer me up.

I go inside and take a seat in the back pew. The priest is just starting to come down the aisle for the start of Mass. Marcus is with him carrying some shaking thing that clicks incense out. It's a weird smell.

When Miracles Can Dream

Kind of like smoke, but sweeter. They only use it at St. Matthew's on holidays. Marcus gives a small wave and a smile as he goes by. I see his mom in another back pew sitting alone. She's wearing some blue lace cloth on her head with flowers on it. She waves me to come over, so I do. Sitting alone makes me feel weird when I don't know anyone else.

I haven't even been to a Mass done in Latin before. I don't understand most of the words beyond a few I know from Christmas songs. But I recognize what the priest is doing and the Church here is cozy and relaxing. For an hour, it helps me forget about Dad and Ally and him having another kid. At least somewhat. It's still hard to focus much. When I'm going up to get Communion, I follow everyone else in kneeling down at the rail, but I am not sure I even remember walking back to my pew or anything that happened before the priest starts processing out. Guess I'm still a little upset.

After they finish the closing hymn, Marcus's mom waits with me.

"Surprised to see you here." She leans in close so she doesn't have to talk loudly. "I figured you'd still be at your dad's store finishing up your big party."

I shrug. "Yeah . . . well, things got a little crazy after you left."

"You want to talk about it?"

I shake my head. "Not really. Is it okay if maybe I hung out a little with Marcus tonight?"

"It's alright with me. Why don't you stay for dinner? Provided you call and let someone know where you are."

I groan and roll my eyes. "Do I really have to call?"

"That's the deal. Maybe if they know you're safe, they'll say it's okay? Whatever happened, maybe your dad needs a night to process it too?"

Marcus comes out. "Hey TJ. It's awesome you came back."

"Yeah. You do Mass nice here."

Marcus's mom puts on her coat and swings her purse over her arm. "Marcus, I got a surprise. I invited TJ for dinner."

"Really? That's awesome." He high-fives me. "I haven't had a friend over in a long time. It'll be lots of fun." His eyes narrow on me. "You look sad. Everything okay?"

I zip up my coat. "Yeah, it's fine. Just had a big fight with my dad. Need to chill somewhere until we can figure things out."

Marcus turns to his mom. "Can TJ sleep over? Sometimes a night away can help people get over whatever made them mad."

She smiles and nods. "It's okay with me if it's okay with TJ's dad."

I don't think a night is going to make Dad cheating on Mom and having a secret family make sense. But I just smile and pretend like it will. Anything to make it so I can at least get one night at a friend's house without having to think about it.

"How about I pick up a pizza? Any recommendations?"

"Lucia's is really good."

"Lucia's it is!"

Marcus's mom loads us into the back seat of a small blue car and drives out of the lot. We stop outside a small Italian place Mom used to take us to. Lucia's had the best pizza and garlic knots in town and people would come from all over the area to try their food.

We go inside and the brick walls and golden wood floors remind me of being there with Mom and Melanie. The Christmas decorations even look the same. The same angel on top of the tree. The same merry-go-round horses riding up and down to old-sounding Christmas songs. I remember leaning against the counter as a kid and watching them. I could do it for hours. Or at least until Mom said our pizza was ready.

Marcus and his mom decide to let me pick the pizza toppings since I'm the guest. I look through the menu and they literally have like a thousand different toppings. I know I don't want any of the gross vegetables on them, but that still leaves a lot of choices. After a lot of help from Marcus and his mom, we settle on white garlic pizza with breaded chicken and that fluffy white cheese that's in ravioli that I can't pronounce the name of.

Francesco

"TJ, why don't you go outside and call your dad?" Marcus's mom raises an eyebrow at me and gives me the stare Mom used to give me when she really wanted me to do something without her asking me again.

"Okay." I sigh as I take out my phone and head outside. Somehow it seems like it got ten degrees colder just since we went inside.

I select Dad's number on the phone. But I don't want to talk to him. I don't want to hear him make excuses for having a baby with someone else. I don't want him to ask me to meet her or to tell me he's sorry or that he loves me. Because it's all lies, and he just wants me to pretend like nothing happened and make him feel better about hurting us. Well I'm not gonna do it. I close my phone and stuff it in my pocket.

I look up and there's Mr. Gabriel. Still dressed like St. Nick and looking more worried than I ever saw him before.

He runs to me. "Oh my gosh, TJ!" He throws his arms around me a second before pushing himself back. "I'm sorry. I shouldn't have hugged you like that. I was just getting worried I'd never find you. I've been looking all over town for you for a few hours now. I was afraid I was going to have to call the police."

"Aren't you supposed to call the police right away?" I raise an eyebrow, secretly glad he didn't. Because I don't want to have some cop force me to come home.

When Miracles Can Dream

He pats me on the head. "I probably should have, but I thought I would be able to find you on my own. And I didn't want to have the police asking a lot of questions about why you ran off."

I shake my head. "So how come you're out here looking for me? Where's Dad?"

"He had an emergency . . ." He clears his throat. "Your sister fell and hurt herself and he drove Ally to the hospital."

Of course he did. I bite my lip and take a step back. "I guess I know where he always is when he's not at the store or not at home. He's with his other family. Guess he loves them more than me."

"That's not true." Mr. Gabriel kneels to eye level with me. "But regardless of how it happened, he does have a daughter and he does love her. That's not wrong, and it's not fair to her to expect him not to love her. I know he shouldn't have kept it a secret like he did, but you need to give him the chance to explain. To make it right."

I push him and shake my head. "No, I don't. And I don't want to hear him tell me why having another family is okay. So if you're here to make me go home, I'm not going. I'm going to a friend's house tonight."

"No, I promised your dad I'd find you and bring you back safe."

I fold my arms. "Just tell him I'm sleeping over a friend's house. If he's really at the hospital, I can't stay at home alone anyway."

Francesco

Mr. Gabriel sighs and adjusts his glasses. "TJ, don't push away your father. He's your family and you won't always have him."

My eyes start burning and I wipe away a tear. "Look, I know you're just trying to help. But you don't get it. You didn't see how much Mom missed him, and you didn't know us yet when Dad wasn't there when the gas leaked. So you don't get it."

"Maybe not, but that doesn't mean I don't know about family problems." He watches a mom and dad and their two kids pass by, dragging a Christmas tree and a bag of decorations to their car. "You can't replace people when you lose them. And you can't get the time back once it's gone. You need to make things right with the people you love while you still have them. Because you don't want things to be bad and then something bad happens to take them away from you." Now his eyes have some tears.

I look in the restaurant window. Looks like the pizza's ready. "I have to go. My friend's mom is gonna let me stay the night. I promise I'll call the store tomorrow. Then I'll figure out what to do. I just . . . don't want to see Dad right now. Thanks for coming to find me. Tell him I'm safe and not to worry."

I go back inside without even waving goodbye. I turn around to look out the window. It's started snowing, and Mr. Gabriel is gone.

When *Miracles* Can *Dream*

Marcus's house is like something out of a Christmas card. It's a small cottage on the edge of town on another street I've never been on before. All of the windows are lined with colored lights. There are small trees in the window and a Nativity Scene in the center. On the lawn, they have a Santa and reindeer and colored stake lights lining the walkway to their porch. Lit garland hangs across the railing of their porch. It's so beautiful. It's like Dad's store, only since it's a home, even better. It must be so nice to live in a house where you can look out and see these lights every day. The falling snow makes it look even prettier.

We get out of the car, and I carry the pizza up the walkway. I look up and take in the snow falling gently on my face. It's dusting the grass and makes everything feel so wintry.

"You okay, man? You need me to help?" Marcus elbows me.

"Nah, just enjoying the snow" I smile and walk up to the door. It doesn't snow that much around here, but when it does, it makes everything so beautiful.

Inside, it looks even more Christmassy than outside. Their tree is the perfect mix of soft colored lights and special ornaments that probably hold special meaning to Marcus and his mom. The fireplace mantle has even more figures and stocking holders with what looks like a likeness of Marcus and his mom in the center.

Francesco

"Where did you even get those?"

Marcus just laughs and eases me into the kitchen. I look on the walls and see pictures of Jesus and Mary and Joseph. One of them is a 3D wood carving of Jesus as a little boy with parents. There are also a lot of pictures of Marcus and his mom from recently. Also lots of him when he was little by himself. One looks like he was about four in it. He's in front of a Christmas tree. He was a cute little kid. Big smile. But I won't dare tell him that. It'll just be weird.

Marcus points to one of him at the altar of that Church in his altar server outfit. He's smiling just as big as when he was a kid. "That was after my first Mass serving. It was awesome, and I was so happy. That was a really good day. Kind of like this."

I put the pizza down on their kitchen table. "What's so good about today?"

He claps me on the back. "I haven't had a friend visit in a long time. I love Mom, but sometimes it's good to have another kid to hang out with."

I feel myself smiling. "Yeah, I guess it is." I can't remember the last time I had dinner at a friend's house. I never seemed good at making friends. Kids didn't bother me too much. I don't think they meant to always ignore me. We all sort of just did our own thing.

Marcus's mom gets out a cranberry soda that's a dark pink in color. She pours us each a glass. I take a sip and it reminds me of a soda I used to drink at

When Miracles Can Dream

Aunt Phyllis's on Christmas Eve. It's sweet and makes me think of Mom and Melanie, but not in a way that makes me sad.

We sit down and pray and then Marcus's mom passes paper plates and we each get a slice. Maybe I'm just enjoying having a friend, but this is the best pizza I ever had. So cheesy and gooey. It makes the soda taste even sweeter, which makes the pizza taste even better.

We talk about our favorite Christmas gifts and movies. And then we talk about our favorite Christmas foods like the mint cookies Marcus's mom would make or Aunt Phyllis's fried dough.

For the first time since the Christmas Eve Mom and Melanie died, I feel like I have a family again.

After dinner, the snow's pretty thick on the ground and still falling. But there's no wind, so it just falls gently. So we convince Marcus's mom to let us go outside and play in the snow.

Marcus grabs a snowball and throws it at me. I laugh as it smashes on my arm. I pick one up too and throw it back, but I miss.

"Need a little help with your pitching?" He sticks his tongue out and throws another. Direct hit.

I run over to him and tackle him to the ground. "Maybe I can't throw a snowball very well, but I can pin you."

Francesco

He flips me and then I flip him.

He breaks free and hits me with another snowball. But this time I have one waiting, and I hit him back. Right in the face. We laugh and make snow angels and even a small snowman. Not a very big one because there isn't enough snow yet. Maybe a snow boy? Snow kid? We'll work on the name later.

When we go back inside, Marcus's mom shouts from the kitchen, "Marcus Tobias, you take those shoes off at the door. Don't you track snow in my living room!"

Marcus laughs. "Uh oh, middle name. She's serious." He laughs again. "We'd better listen."

I laugh too and kick off my shoes.

We trade our wet, snowy clothes for pajamas. They let me borrow one of Marcus's. It fits perfectly. I never realized we were exactly the same size. Marcus's are white with red snowflakes and mine are white with green trimming and holly. Very Christmassy.

When we go downstairs, Marcus's mom has a cup of hot chocolate waiting for each of us. She puts on *Home Alone* and we sip our hot chocolate with nothing but the fireplace, the Christmas lights, and the TV for light. I love when hot chocolate has whipped cream and marshmallows in it. And I think there's even a little bit of mint in it. But just a little, because I can barely taste it.

After the movie, Marcus's mom goes up to bed, but he convinces her to let us sleep down here under the

When Miracles Can Dream

Christmas tree. We get pillows and blankets and make it so soft and comfy. A Christmas fort! The Christmas lights make it so relaxing and make me feel like I'm six years old again and waiting for Santa.

Marcus is asleep fast. He snores a little, and I chuckle.

I stay awake a little longer, just looking at the Christmas lights and the pictures on the wall. I wonder if Marcus misses his dad sometimes. He doesn't talk about him, but he doesn't seem sad like I do. I wish I could be as cool as he is about things. Maybe then I wouldn't be so sad.

I stare at the tree and remember how beautiful ours used to be, and I keep staring until my eyes get heavy and I dream of Mom.

Chapter 10
Micah

11:15 PM

The clock on the wall taunts me. I don't remember the last time I looked at a face clock. At the store, the time is always readily displayed on my phone or a computer screen. And I don't think I've even been home long enough to sit and watch a clock. I never realized quite how slow a minute passes. It's like these face clocks literally slow down time, that second hand creeping its way around the face.

I shut my eyes for a moment, but I feel like I could do anything but sleep right now.

I open my eyes and look up. Ally sleeps like a baby next to Kelsey. Poor thing crashed like a toddler around 9PM. Kelsey hasn't woken up since the fall. The doctors said she has a mild concussion, but they can't explain why she hasn't woken up yet.

I lean in and caress her face. I think of how happy she is every time she sees me. Even now, her mouth seems curved into the slightest smile. She has a smile for everyone. She deserves better than to be some dark secret her father keeps in the back of his closet.

I think of Theo, how confused he must be right now. He doesn't even understand all of what happened, I don't think. He doesn't need to. He knows I betrayed his mother. I betrayed him. Even if I didn't know it at the time, I betrayed my son. And now, an innocent girl is forever caught in between my sin and my heart.

Feeling a cramp in my legs, I get up and walk out of the room, pacing nervously down the hall. I stop at a water fountain to get a drink, but it hardly seems a match for the burning in my chest. As I walk past each room, I see the light on each one. I think of the stories of each patient here and wonder if their lives could possibly be as big a mess as I've made mine.

Then I look up and see Janny standing by the elevators.

"What are you . . . it's almost midnight."

She shrugs. "I wanted to see how you were doing."

We take a seat. "I'm hanging in. They let you in?"

"I manage a store. I think I can swing getting around visiting hours."

The faintest of chuckles escapes. "Ed called earlier. Said he found Theo and that he was staying at a friend's house. It's probably for the best. I don't want him home alone, and I don't want him staying in a hospital all night."

She takes my hand. "What about Kelsey?"

"The doctors say, in theory, she should be fine. But she hasn't woken up yet, and that's concerning them."

She squeezes my hand and looks me in the eye. "Micah, you'll get through this. She'll be okay."

My eyes burn as I lean back into the chair. "Janny, I've just screwed everything up so badly. And I don't know how to fix it."

"Have you tried being honest?"

I shake my head. "I cheated on my wife. I spent ten years trying to keep these two worlds from colliding. And today I finally failed."

"You messed up, and I know that had very long-term consequences. But has trying to keep it secret gotten you anywhere? Theo is real. Kelsey is real. They are both your children, and they both need their father. Kelsey has special needs. She's always going to need someone to advocate for her. And Theo? Theo's still grieving the loss of his mother and sister. And I know you may not like hearing this, but you've been emotionally absent from him. Secrets haven't gotten you anywhere, Micah. Maybe now that everything's out in the open, this is your chance to really make things right. There's a lot of anger to sort through, but now you're free from the secret. This is your chance to fix things."

I get up and walk to Kelsey's room. I look in through the doorway and just stare at her. How could something so beautiful have come from something so wrong? So hurtful to people I love!

"How can I make Theo understand when I don't understand myself?"

She comes up behind me and puts her hand on my shoulder. "Maybe that's the next step, then. You need to come to terms with your life. And maybe then, you can help Theo do the same."

She turns to go.

Francesco

I take her hand. "Janny, wait."

She spins around and for just a second, we stand frozen, staring into each other. Tensions I can almost physically feel, that I haven't felt since I looked into my wife's eyes.

She takes a step back. "You're not in the right place, Micah. But I'm not going anywhere. When you're ready . . . we'll see."

She walks to the elevator and pushes the "down" button.

"Janny."

She turns and looks back.

"Thank you. For today. For everything."

The door opens with a ding and she steps inside.

And I'm alone again with nothing but heart monitors to pierce the silence of the hospital.

11:22 PM

5:23 AM

I don't remember exactly when I fell asleep. I just remember opening my eyes to see that almost 6 hours had passed since I last took note of the clock. I suppose I could do worse sleeping on a night like this.

Kelsey is still in her bed. Ally is awake, but still quiet. Just stroking Kelsey's hair and fighting back tears. I dare not approach her and try to talk. Because right now, I don't think anything I could say would make her feel any better.

When *Miracles* Can *Dream*

The elevator doors open and Ed steps out, carrying a paper bag. He's already dressed as Santa.

I get up to meet him. "It's Sunday, Ed. You did a lot yesterday. You can have the day off."

Ed laughs. "Santa doesn't get a day off during the busy season." He takes out a foam container. "I brought you some take-out from one of my favorite breakfast spots."

I chuckle and take it. "Thanks, Ed." I look inside and pull out a wrapped breakfast burrito. "Looks good."

Ed takes a seat next to me. "Well it tastes better. Don't just do that trick where you look at food until it turns rotten. You need to eat so you don't pass out."

I unwrap the burrito and hold it up in mock salute before taking a bite. It's actually pretty darn good, but my mind can't process "good food" right now.

"How are they doing?" Ed takes off his glasses and wipes them with a cloth.

"Kelsey's still not awake. I don't know what to think. The doctors have so many opinions and what-ifs. I just want my little girl to wake up so I can tell her I'm sorry." I take another bite and set the burrito down. "Thank you for making sure Theo got somewhere safe."

Ed shrugs. "I don't think I did much. He pretty much arranged his own place to stay and told me how it was going to be." He laughs. "I'll call him later to see what we do next. He can't stay at a friend's house indefinitely."

"I know." My stomach knots, and my arms throb. "I need to talk to him. I just don't know what to say. I've spent his whole life hiding from him, and now I almost feel like we're strangers."

Ed leans in closer. "Micah, I wasn't entirely honest with you before. In our interview."

"What do you mean?"

"When I said I didn't have a family . . . it wasn't entirely true. I had a family. Once. Like you. I married the most beautiful girl in my school. Her name was Evelyn. My Evy. We were high school sweethearts. We traveled all over the country. We ate at so many great restaurants, and we were so happy. I wasn't always this outgoing, you know. I used to be a lot more quiet and reserved."

"Hard to picture you reserved."

"Seems like another life to me," he says.

"It's a struggle for me every day to force myself to be outgoing for the sake of the store."

"Evy could make me sing in front of the world. I wasn't afraid of anything as long as I was with her."

I stare into Ed's eyes and notice tears forming. "Ed, you don't have to talk about this if it's going to upset you. We were strangers. You weren't obliged to tell me about your wife. We've all lost someone we loved. I get where you're going with this, but it's okay."

He shakes his head. "I don't think you do. Allow me to finish." He swallows hard and lets out an extended sigh. "There was one thing that kept us from truly having that perfect life. One dark cloud. We couldn't get pregnant. We tried. We saw doctors. Took some medications to try and help. It was almost a decade together and still . . . no baby. We considered adopting. We even agreed to do it. We just never seemed to get around to it. But then . . . a miracle happened. Evy was in for a routine checkup and they found out she was pregnant. We were so happy. We prepared a nursery and had a shower. All the usual things, and our family was finally going to be complete. Her pregnancy was smooth. No major complications. Nothing scary. Not until she went into delivery. I don't even understand to this day what happened. I just know they took her away and when they came out . . . she was gone. The doctor explained it all to me, but all I could hear was that my Evy was gone."

"Ed . . ." I reach out and take his hand. "I'm sorry."

"But my boy was alive." Ed smiles. "Somehow, they were able to save the baby. He was beautiful. He was perfect. Not a thing wrong. My boy, my Toby."

I smile. I remember that feeling. As guilty as I was, I was always awestruck at how beautiful my children were when they were born. So perfect.

Ed wipes aside a tear. "He was perfect, but my Evy was gone. And I could never get over it. I didn't hate my son. I loved him. I didn't yell at him for it, but there was always a wall. Always a barrier. Something to keep me from embracing life with him and enjoying it. So many times, he wanted to do something with me, and I wasn't able to give it my time. Because I was just so sad that my Evy wasn't there to share it with us. I let my grief rob me of the time I had with him. And we don't get that time back."

"Do you still talk to him?"

Ed gets quiet and tenses his hands. "I lost him too. Eleven years of time I was gifted by God with a beautiful son, and in one night, one stupid accident . . . I lost him too. Forever. I buried him next to his mother and . . . for a while, I felt like I was even more in a daze. But then it dawned on me how it was my grief for Evy that kept me from enjoying the life I had with Toby. And I decided I wasn't going to give that grief any more of my life. It had taken enough." Ed straightens himself up. "I was going to help people. I was going to use my life to bring joy to others, to children. Being 'Santa' may not be the most prestigious gig, but it brings children legitimate joy. And I think that makes it one of the most worthwhile."

My mouth hangs open and I try to say something. But I don't know what. Everything that comes to mind seems so trite. So meaningless.

Ed takes my hand. "Your son is growing up. There's more than one way to lose a son. Don't let yours be lost to time. He's young. There's still time to develop a relationship with him, but that time is slipping fast.

He needs his father to be his father. Don't let your fears and regrets cause you to make more."

As Ed gets up to leave, I just sit there in silence, his words swirling in my head. I pray that it already isn't too late to build a relationship with Theo. I saw the look in his eyes when he heard what I'd done. Maybe before, I could have repaired what we have. But now, I might have just missed the last chance I had.

Chapter 11
TJ

When I open my eyes, I'm back home. I can smell banana chip pancakes cooking, just like Mom used to make me on my birthday. The sun is shining even brighter than usual with the snow on the ground.

I get up and follow the smell into the kitchen, where Marcus is helping his mom set the table.

"Good morning, TJ," he says. "Mom made us breakfast so you're not hungry before we take you back to the store."

"Do we have to go?" I take a seat, rubbing my eyes and trying to hang on to the fading feeling of being with Mom and Melanie again.

Marcus's mom flips some pancakes onto a plate and puts it down in front of me. "It was wonderful to have you over, TJ. But you do have to go back home. I'm sure your dad misses you."

"I doubt it."

Marcus takes a seat opposite me. "Come on, TJ. Give him a chance. I don't know what happened yesterday after we left to make you two fight, but you gotta talk to him and work it out. You shouldn't stay mad at your dad."

I shrug. I don't want to fight with them. They were nice to me and gave me a fun night. I know I can't stay here forever. I just wish I could stay here until after Christmas.

Francesco

The pancakes are as good as Mom's were. I try to imagine she's the one who made them. Imagine how it feels to be six again. When Mom was alive and I had a little sister. Then I try to enjoy this moment, where I have a friend and am part of a family for at least one more day.

I wave goodbye to Marcus and his mom as they pull away from the store. I take a deep breath before turning to go inside, where I know I'll be yelled at for running away.

I walk into the store. It's pretty crowded already, but it always is this time of year.

I look around. I see several of the workers I know, but I don't see Dad. Or even Janny.

"TJ!" Mr. Gabriel's voice.

I spin around and see him. He runs to me, but stops just short of hugging me. "You're back. I'm so glad."

I kick my feet together. "I told you I was going to be fine."

He nods. "You did."

"Where's Dad?"

"Something happened after you ran off. Your father had an emergency regarding . . ." He motions me to the back and I follow. "I don't know how much you heard yesterday and honestly, it isn't my place to tell you. But you and your father should have a long talk about it. I can call him, and maybe he can come get you."

I shake my head. "Let me just help you today. I don't wanna talk to him."

I quickly change into my elf costume and meet Mr. Gabriel out in Santa's workshop. He's already at Santa's throne. I go next to him and grab some candy canes to hand to the kids coming to see him.

He pats me on the shoulder. "TJ, please. Don't shut out the people who love you. Especially not your dad."

I twirl a candy cane on my finger. "Dad's the one who's shut me out. Since I was little. Now that I know his secret, he wants me to just forget all about it so he feels better. Well, I'm not gonna do it."

Mr. Gabriel sighs. "I know. And he made a mistake. I think he realizes that now. I made the same mistake. I had a little boy once. Toby. He was a lot like you. Kind, quiet, considerate. But I felt guilty and regretted something, and it caused me to not give him the love he needed. Then one day, something bad happened to him, and he died. And then all of the reasons I didn't give him every bit of love I could have, they didn't seem to matter anymore. You and your dad have been through a lot. I know a lot of it hurts. But don't let the hurt keep you from experiencing the love. Your dad didn't take the chance in the past, but now the ball's in your court to give him one more chance. Don't be the reason you'll have regrets one day about the time you didn't get to share."

Francesco

I nod to get him to leave me alone. He's a nice old man, but he doesn't know how it is for me and Dad.

They let the kids start coming in. One by one, they make a line until they're halfway across the store.

They tell Mr. Gabriel what they want for Christmas. Some have a long list of toys. Others just want their dad to come home for Christmas. I know how they feel.

When I look up from my lunch, I see Dad standing there. His eyes are full of tears, and I can see in them that he's happy to see me and also upset at seeing me. Kind of like he's always looked at me.

"Theo, I'm so glad you're back."

I sip my Sprite and pretend he's not there.

He takes a seat at the table next to me. "It doesn't have to be now, but we need to talk about all of this."

"Why?" I shoot him angry eyes. "What's talking about it going to do? You hurt Mom."

He tenses his lips and looks away. "Don't you think I know that? I spent the rest of her life trying to make up for it. What I did was wrong, and I don't make any excuses for it. But that's not going to change that I'm still your father, and I still love you."

"Then why can't you look at me? Why couldn't you ever look at me?" I get up to go but he grabs my hand and turns me to him.

"I am looking at you," he says.

We lock eyes and I try not to cry.

"Right now, I am looking at my son. I see you, Theo."

I shake my head. "Look at me without being sad. Look at me without seeing another mistake. Look at me like someone who doesn't remind you that you hurt Mom. Because that's all I see. That's all I ever saw. I never understood what it was, why every time you looked at me, I felt like I did something wrong. Like me just being here hurts you." I break free of his grip. "Now I do. Now I get it."

"I'm sorry."

I stop and turn my head down so he doesn't see me crying.

I feel his hand on my shoulder. "You don't deserve to feel what you're feeling. Over my mistakes. And I know I haven't done the best job of making you feel wanted. But I do love you, Theo. Even if I have to learn to show it better. When I thought I lost you with Mom and your sister that night, it didn't hurt any less losing you than losing them. When I saw you alive in that hospital bed, as much as I ached like hell for Mom and Melanie, I was so relieved that you were okay." He gulps and exhales a hard breath that's cold on my neck. "I was in a fire when I was a kid. I was just a bit younger than you were when I almost lost you. I don't even remember where I was. Somewhere with a lot of singing, I think. I remember Christmas songs and decorations, but it wasn't the store. I remember

Francesco

this kid was talking to me about something, and I remember seeing all the big Nativity statues. And then I remember how big the flames were and how scared I was. I was coughing because the smoke was choking me. And I remember feeling someone pick me up and push me close to their chest. Just like you do. Someone saved me. Someone carried me out of that burning building and set me on the ground where I could breathe again."

I feel my stomach twist thinking of that night, of that man who saved me, of seeing Melanie lying next to me. Dead. "Why are you telling me this? Why now?"

"Because of what happened after. I always remember being scared of my dad. He was cold at times, hard on me. Wanted me to learn how to be a real man. But after that . . . he changed. I think almost losing me scared him. And from then on, he made an effort, even if he had to still be a little hard on me, to let me know that he loved me. I heard later on a couple of people died in that fire. Even other kids. It was bad and people always said how lucky I was to make it out. He could've lost me and that shook him to his very core. I never quite understood that until the night I almost lost you. Only I didn't do as good a job at showing you how much I loved you. I failed you, because unlike my dad, I had another big mistake hanging over us. I did something that betrayed your mother. And it was wrong. But the baby that came from that mistake, she's still real. And she doesn't deserve to be abandoned because of how she came to be. She needs me too. And I love her too. How could I not? She's still my daughter. She's your sister. And I know, right now, you're angry. You're right to be. I shouldn't have kept her a secret. She didn't deserve that, and neither did you. But at some point, you and I need to figure out how we all can move forward and be something resembling a family again. And I know now, that will have to include her. She's hurt right now, Theo. She won't wake up. The doctors say her head could be hurt a lot worse than we thought. But she's still in there, and she needs the both of us. She didn't hurt you or Mom. Whatever you think about me, she's innocent in all of this."

I turn to him and we're both crying. And I want to run to him and hug him and feel like everything could be okay again.

Then I remember how on that last night, Mom kept looking at the door. Waiting, holding back a tear. How maybe, if he were there, he could've gotten all of us out alive. And we'd still be together. And he wasn't there. Not because he had to work. That was a lie. He was there because he was kissing someone who wasn't Mom.

"You know," I swallow hard. "I think Mom knew. I think she knew and never said anything. Because that's how she was. She wanted to keep us all together as a family. So much that she would even just pretend that she didn't know, just so you and her wouldn't have to fight. Well, I'm not going to pretend that what you did is okay. So if your other family needs you so much, you should go be with them. I don't need you. I know how to take care of myself. I don't need you. I'll be fine."

"Theo, you can't stay by yourself."

"I have friends."

"No." He shakes his head. "We'll think of something to make this work, but I want to know where you are. Because regardless of what you think or how mad you are, I'm your father. And it's time both of us started remembering that."

I take off my elf hat and toss it. If Dad wasn't ready to be there before, I'm not just going to pretend that it's okay for him to pretend like everything's going to be okay now.

As the sun goes down and the lights go on in our outside light trails, I think of Mom. She designed so many of these. Even if we've changed some of the bulbs over the years and replaced some broken parts, a lot of these designs are still based on her ideas. She always kept the house pretty at Christmas. And the store too. I miss these lights so much. Even if I can see them here, it's just not the same. But at least I can still sort of feel close to her when I see the colored lights against the starry sky.

When Miracles Can Dream

I sit back on one of the benches along the trail, and a cold wind blows against my face and makes the streams of tears on my face feel extra cold.

I think of Marcus and his mom. How happy they seem. How happy I was spending time with them. How good it felt to play with another kid my age. Even if it was while wrestling, how it felt good to feel another person's arms around me again. Someone who cared, even a little.

I go through every moment I can remember of Dad when Mom was alive. I try to think of a time when I felt he loved me. I never thought he didn't love me until after Mom died. I just thought he was always busy because of the store. Thinking back now, every time he was late, every time he was too tired to play with me, it all seems different. Like he was trying to not see me because he was thinking about how he hurt Mom. And how I reminded him.

"He does love you, TJ."

Mom?

I look up, and I can see her standing there with Christmas lights behind her for a second. Like she's an angel.

Then I look closer, and I see that it's just Janny.

"You look disappointed," she says. She takes a seat next to me.

I shrug. "No, I'm just thinking."

"Did you hear what I said? Your dad loves you. I know a lot of this is confusing right now. And maybe he's not been the best at navigating this. But he does care. Even if you're angry at him right now, you should give him a chance sooner or later."

I sigh. "All Mom wanted was for him to be with us. And she died without him because he was with his other family."

"What he did was wrong, but that doesn't mean you should never forgive him either. Just because the things we're angry about were bad things doesn't mean that anger doesn't hurt you even more. I never met your mom, but from what I can tell about her from you and your dad, she'd want you to have a happy life. Even if she wasn't in it anymore. She wouldn't want you spending your lives being angry or apologizing."

I tighten myself on the bench and fold my arms. Mom always said stuff like that.

"Do you like my dad?"

Her mouth drops and she moves back. "Well, he's a good man and a good boss."

"You know that's not what I mean. I'm not as dumb as you think. I know about love and things. I don't just mean liking him like you like a friend or the guy who works at the store. I mean do you want to kiss him? Marry him?"

She chuckles and exhales. "TJ, grown-up relationships are complicated."

I shake my head. "Yeah, Dad loves that word. Complicated. It means I'm right, but you don't want to tell me that I'm right."

She takes my hand. "'Complicated' means that there isn't an easy yes or no answer. Yes, I'd like there to be more to our relationship than just him being my boss. I think he's a genuinely good man, with a truly good heart." She turns my head up. "And a wonderful son."

I laugh. "Sounds like an easy 'yes' to me."

"It's not. Your father's still in a bad place. He misses your mom and still feels guilty about pretty much every choice he's ever made. He's not in a place where he can look at finding love again. Before he can do that, he needs to make peace with the past."

I kick my feet together and try to think of what it would be like to have Janny be my "new Mom." For some reason, I don't hate the idea as much as I do Dad kissing Aunt Phyllis's nurse. Maybe because I know Mom would want Dad to move on and be happy with someone else. That's very different from him kissing someone while she was still alive.

"If he did make peace with the past, like you say, would you want to date him then?"

She gets silent for a moment and puts her arm around me. "The only thing I'll say is that if anyone gets the privilege of being a stepmom to you, they'll be a very lucky woman."

I feel myself smile. It feels good and yet it also makes me feel guilty for getting to smile instead of being mad at Dad for Mom.

Francesco

"That said . . ." She takes my hand. "Your dad asked if I could let you stay with me tonight. He doesn't want you home alone, and he doesn't want you staying with friends he hasn't met. But he doesn't want to leave your sister for too long. At least not until she wakes up."

I nod. "I get it. If she's hurt, he should stay with her. Do you know how she's doing?"

"She hasn't woken up yet from her fall. The doctors are doing tests to find out why."

"Even though I'm still mad at Dad, I do want her to get better. None of this is her fault." The tears start coming again, and I wipe them aside with my sleeve. "I don't know what to do. I just wish everything could be normal again." I throw my head on her chest and let her hold me as I cry. And for just a second, it's like Mom is holding me again too.

Chapter 12
TJ

Before I know it, it's only a few days 'til Christmas.

I'm staying with Janny in her little cottage on the edge of town. It's painted red and she decorated it with simple Christmas lights on her window. It looks really good with the snow on the ground that paints all the trees around it white.

Her couch is actually more comfy than my bed. It's soft, and I can just sink into the cushions. Especially when she has a fireplace running. It helps me sleep.

Dad doesn't come back to the store much. Janny and Mr. Gabriel run things pretty well, though. Customers come in like crazy every day, but we still manage to leave at a normal time. Sometimes Janny takes me out for dinner at Lucia's. Or we get Chinese takeout.

It's just gotten dark out, and Janny tells me to wait up front while she goes over a few things with the night manager. Then we'll go home and maybe watch *A Christmas Story*.

As I stand by the door watching our motion-sensing dancing and singing elf toy perform for some customers, I see Marcus come into the store.

"Hey, man. Haven't seen you for a few days." I run to greet him. "Last-minute shopping?"

He smiles, but I can see some tears in his eyes. He shakes his head. "Not exactly."

"What's wrong?"

He sighs. "Just found out we got reassigned. Mom got word this morning. They want her to go down to Georgia."

"Georgia? That's not fair." My stomach knots and twists. The one time I had a friend and now this happens.

He shrugs. "I'm used to it. But this was our first home, and it was nice to have a friend. I know we'll be back, but not for a while. I just wanted to find you and say goodbye before it happened."

"Wait, you're not leaving tonight, are you?"

"After Christmas. But I didn't want to wait until then. With all the craziness, I might not get a chance."

I look around. "I still need to get you a Christmas gift."

He chuckles. "And you called me a last-minute shopper."

I pocket my hands. "Yeah, well . . . I've had a ton going on."

He nods. "Yeah, I know. Don't worry about getting me a gift. For real. It's just been fun having someone to hang with these past few weeks. It's been a while since I've had a new friend. But TJ?"

"Yeah?"

"Your dad? Whatever's going on with you and him, you should go to him and try to fix it. Like right now. It's almost Christmas. You shouldn't be mad at your family on Christmas. You should be with your family. The ones who love you."

I kick my feet together. "It's not that simple, man."

"Of course it is." He puts his hand on my shoulder. "Don't you think I miss my dad every day? Don't waste time being angry. Believe me, it's not worth it."

I nod. "Maybe you're right. Maybe once Dad gets back from the hospital, we'll talk."

He shakes his head. "Go right now. Don't wait."

"Why do you care so much, man? And why now?"

Marcus wipes aside a tear. "Look, you're my friend. I don't want you to be alone for Christmas. I want you to be with your family. Especially if I'm not here. You know better than anyone that you don't know what's going to happen tomorrow."

He reaches out and hugs me. Not even a bro hug. A real, tight hug. Like the kind I gave Melanie. Then he pulls back and turns to go. "It's Christmas, TJ. Don't choose to spend it alone." Then he waves and walks out the door. Funny thing is, seeing my friend walk away after saying that pounds my chest, and I feel more alone than ever.

As Janny and I go to drive home, I think of asking her to go see Dad. Marcus's words swirl in my head. I wonder why he and his dad aren't talking. Did his dad walk away? Do something bad? Or maybe he's dead too, and Marcus just doesn't like talking about it.

Francesco

Then I think of Mom and Melanie, and how much I wish I could go back to that Christmas Eve when they died and warn them to get out.

Then I remember a time when I was a little boy and Dad came into my room, thinking I was asleep. He sang me some lullaby I can't remember the words to. Just the melody. I hum it softly to myself. I hadn't thought about that in years, and now I can see it as clear as if it just happened.

"That's a pretty song," Janny says. "Where's it from?"

I stare out the window at the buildings passing by, all decorated in Christmas lights. "Just something from when I was a kid." I watch as some kids have a snowball fight. It's starting to snow again. It's snowed a lot this year. More than it has in a while. It makes the ground extra pretty, but Janny has to drive a lot slower because the roads are slippery.

We stop at Grand Sun restaurant, a Chinese buffet I used to go to with Mom. It had tons of food and we could eat as much as we wanted. Inside it was always very colorful with lots of red and blue lights, making the place feel like it was always having a party. They really went all out on decorating for Christmas too. Lots of Christmas trees and hanging garland over the chairs. Didn't know the people who ran the Chinese restaurants were so big on Christmas.

Janny and I aren't too hungry so we decide to get the takeout option instead of the buffet. They give

When *Miracles* Can *Dream*

us each a foam container to fill up with whatever we want. Janny gets some of the saucy noodles and the chicken with broccoli. I don't like the broccoli, so I get the noodles with honey chicken. And an eggroll too. Then we get this banana pudding for dessert. We bring the containers to the register, and they weigh them to see how much we have to pay. Then they bag it all up, and we go back to the car.

I swear we were only inside for like ten minutes, but the ground seems like five inches of snow fell in that time. It's really coming down now.

Janny's car slips and slides just a little as she turns out of the parking lot, but it's smooth going once we are on the road.

The food smells good. The smell of Chinese food always makes me think of Mom and being little again.

Luckily, it isn't too far to Janny's cottage. She pulls into her driveway and we trudge to the house, snow crunching under our feet. The walkway is slippery, and both Janny and I almost fall walking to the house, but we catch each other so we each stay standing.

We go inside and Janny turns on her Christmas lights so they are the only lights in her house. It's beautiful and makes our dinner feel so special, eating it in front of the TV while Ralphie asks for his BB gun.

After we're done eating and the movie is in its last act, I lean my head in and rest it on Janny's shoulder. She pulls a quilt over me and strokes my head. For a second, I can close my eyes and pretend that everything that's ever happened to make me sad was all just a nightmare. That everybody I love is here with me. And for a second, when I open my eyes and see the Christmas lights, I almost believe it's real. As I think of what Marcus said about Dad, I think I'd give anything if we could be a real family again.

After the movie's over, I clear our trash and put all of it into a big bag. Then I take our glasses to the sink and wash them with soap and hot water.

"You didn't have to do that, TJ." Janny pats me on the head. "I would've gotten it."

"That's okay. You're letting me stay here, so I have to help out. Dinner was very good. Thank you."

She smiles. "Well, I'm glad you're having a good time. It's been good to have some time to get to know you a little better."

I nod. "Yeah, it's been good."

"TJ? Do you think tomorrow, maybe we can call your dad? I know it doesn't seem like it right now because of him staying at the hospital to be with your . . . to be with Kelsey. But he really is trying. Can't you give him a chance to show that to you?"

I turn off the water and stare for a moment. Not at anything in particular. Just . . . thinking. I really want her to be right. I want Dad to be trying. But it's so hard to imagine that when, my whole life, it seemed like he felt being my dad was a punishment.

When Miracles Can Dream

I grab the trash bag and step into my shoes again. "I'll think about it."

"TJ, the trash can wait until tomorrow."

I slip on my coat. "No, I got it." I push out the front door. The wind's really gotten bad. Snow blows in my face and the cold cuts through all of my clothes.

I turn my head down and trudge toward the trashcans and toss the bag in.

Then I turn to go back inside. I make it up two of the steps to the porch before my feet catch a patch of ice and then everything spins.

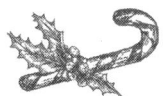

"TJ!" Janny's voice is just below a scream. I hear her running to my side as snow falls on my face.

She helps me to my feet. A really sharp pain shoots through my leg all the way through to my foot. I try not to scream, but I feel from the cold wind on my face that I must be crying.

We go into the house and she sits me down on a kitchen chair. She rolls down my sock and looks at my ankle. She touches it and feels around. That makes it hurt more. I wince and clench my fists.

"I told you not to go out in this." She rolls the sock back up. "I should get you to a doctor. Could be a sprain, but it's pretty swollen."

"But you can't drive in this. It's bad out there. I'll be fine." I try to stand up, but the pain is too much and I fall.

Francesco

Janny catches me and sits me back down. "Yeah, well, it was too bad for you to go out there just to throw out some stupid trash that could've waited until tomorrow. I can handle a little snow. I just want to get your ankle looked at. And I don't even know if you hit your head. You're going to the ER."

She gets up to get her coat and I sit there, mad at myself for going out just to end our conversation about Dad. I'm tired and want to go to bed. I don't want to spend all night in a hospital to have them tell me to put ice on my leg. I can just put snow on it in that case. I'm even more bummed I'll probably be hobbling around with a sore leg through Christmas now. This sucks.

Janny comes back bundled up and keys in hand. "Alright, give me your hand and I'll help you get to the car."

She gently pulls me up from my seat and we walk out the front door. The steps outside are even more slick now, but she keeps me from falling and we make it to the car.

She sits me down in the back seat and props my leg up with random stuff she has back there like a shopping bag of knick-knacks and a folded blanket.

Then she gets into the driver's seat and starts the car. At first the car doesn't move. But after a good rev, it begins to crunch through the snow. Janny slowly plows through to the end of the driveway and turns onto the main road.

When Miracles Can Dream

Nobody else seems to be out now. I guess everyone decided to stay home because of all the snow.

Janny looks back at me in the mirror. "You doing okay, TJ?"

"Yeah." A grunt escapes my mouth as pain shoots up my ankle.

"We'll be there soon. I promise. They haven't plowed the roads yet, so I can't go too fast."

"It's okay. I'll be fine."

The snow is so heavy now, I can barely even see the trees or the Christmas lights on the houses anymore. Janny's windshield wipers brush as much of the snow away as they can, but it comes back almost as fast as it can be cleared.

Then two bright lights cut through the snow and I hear a loud horn. And then the worst clang I heard in my entire life. And then screaming.

I open my eyes and the cold pierces into them like a knife. I look around, and I'm in the water. I look over and see Janny's car half on the shore and half in the creek. We must've gone off the road and into the Brickwood Creek.

"Janny!" I look around and try to find her, but I don't see her anywhere. I hope she isn't in the water.

I try to get to the shore, but the water is so cold, and the snow and wind is still strong. Everything is so freezing that I can barely even feel anything on my body at all. Except my leg, which still seems to hurt despite me not even being able to feel anything else but cold.

I flap around until I get closer to the shore. The water isn't too deep. Little by little, the shore gets closer.

I hear Marcus's voice in my head telling me to go see Dad. I should've listened. Then none of this would've happened. I think of how much fun we had together these past few weeks, and how good it was to have a friend. To be part of a real family again.

I hear Janny's voice telling me that my dad is trying. How I should give him another chance. I don't believe it at all, but somehow he's the one I want to see the most right now.

I think of Mr. Gabriel and the sad look in his eyes when he talked about the family he lost.

I think of Aunt Phyllis, and how sad she'd be coming to my funeral.

I think of Kelsey, and how I wish I could've gotten to meet her. I don't even know what she looks like, and she's my sister.

I think of Mom and Melanie, and how great it'd be to see them again.

Then I think about how cold everything is and how sleepy I am.

Chapter 13
Micah

December 22 11:00 PM

Theo's spent the past ten or so days staying with Janny. Her cottage may be small, but according to her, he's happy to stay on her sofa. "At least she has a Christmas tree," he says.

Kelsey still hasn't woken up from her coma yet. *Coma.* The doctors finally started using that word after five days avoiding it. They took her into surgery at least twice now. One to fix a brain bleed or something, and the other I am not even quite sure. I was there when they were explaining it, but I didn't understand it half as well as Ally. I followed her lead since she's the one with medical training.

As I watch her now, I hear my own voice. "Please God..." I don't even know exactly what I want to pray for anymore. For me to get the courage to treat her as part of my family, as my daughter? For her to make a full recovery? For her to just open her eyes?

I look over at Ally, taking Kelsey's hand and gently stroking our little girl's bandaged head.

I take Kelsey's hand and kiss it. "I'm so sorry. I'm sorry that I wasn't strong enough to give you the love you deserved."

Ally looks over at me. "It's not too late, you know. I know my baby girl is still in there. She's not dead."

Francesco

"I know," I say. My hand shakes as I caress Kelsey's face. "I just wish I knew a way to give everyone I love what they need without hurting someone else I love."

"Have you talked to Theo? Maybe now that some time has passed, he'll be more willing to consider coming here? I don't know him very well, but he seems like a good kid. Phyllis is always singing his praises. I think he's going to want to have a relationship with his sister, regardless of how she got here. He was just angry, and I understand that."

"Theo's a good kid. He's angry at me. Once he calms down and realizes that Kelsey is innocent in all of this, he'll want to protect her. He was protective of and very good to Melanie. He'd be no different to Kelsey."

Ally clutches a picture of Kelsey as a baby. "When they told me she had Down Syndrome, I didn't know what to think. I already loved her so much. How could I hold it against her that her childhood would be harder than for other kids? It wasn't her fault. She didn't deserve any less love because of the challenges she faced. And you know what? When I see the love in her eyes when she sees another kid or her gentleness with animals, I know she is exactly how God wanted her to be. She's a better person than me. Sometimes I think it's because of her challenges, not in spite of them."

"You're a good person too." I offer her a smile. "You rose to the challenge of raising a child with special needs, no matter what it cost you. And you did it with only half-hearted support from me. You deserved better than I gave you, and for what little it's worth, I'm sorry. And I need to do better. No excuses."

We both take one of Kelsey's hands and give them a squeeze. Just a reminder to let her know that we're there, just waiting for her to open her eyes.

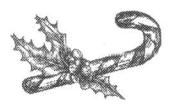

I go down to the cafeteria. Somehow, I'm surprised that it's closed, even though it's after 11 and the hospital is a legitimate ghost town. I guess I just hoped to see something normal for a change. I love spending time with Kelsey, even if she isn't conscious yet. But spending so much time inside that hospital room is getting to me. I'm starting to forget what being somewhere normal feels like.

Ally fell asleep next to Kelsey. I can't sleep. My mind's spinning too much. I don't want to wake Ally, though, so I decided to stretch my legs for a little bit.

As I turn to go back to the elevator, I see Ed turn a corner.

"You're here this late?"

Ed shrugs. "Couldn't sleep."

"How are you even allowed to still be here? I have a child who's a patient. What's your excuse?" I chuckle.

Ed laughs and gestures to his Santa suit. "This might have something to do with it. Some of the kids can't sleep so I was paying them a visit. I've done it for the past few years now, and the hospital staff knows me pretty well. Sometimes when it's late at night, and you're a kid alone in a hospital, seeing Santa can be the best thing in the world."

"I'll bet." I think back to my own time in the hospital as a kid, after the fire. They didn't let my parents stay overnight, and I remember how cold and alone I felt. Ed's got a point. It would've been a big help if Santa could've somehow paid me a visit that Christmas Eve night all those years ago.

Ed takes a seat and exhales deeply.

"You okay?" I sit next to him.

He nods. "Yeah, this time of year just makes me a little anxious. Especially when it's quiet."

"Santa gets anxious at Christmastime?" I shake my head.

Ed laughs. "Kind of strange, isn't it? I guess life's nothing if not ironic. I love what I do. I get to help a lot of people. But I also get to meet a lot of people in their darkest places. If a kid's here this time of year, it could be for something as simple as a tonsillectomy. Or it could be because they're getting really hard cancer treatments. Or they're badly injured. Sometimes from an accident. Sometimes from somebody hurting them. Spending so much time in that darkness takes its toll on you. Even though, helping people . . . I wouldn't have it any other way."

When Miracles Can Dream

I hear the crash of doors opening. My stomach sinks, and I don't even know why. But somehow, I look over and see them wheeling her in. Janny!

I dash over. "Janny! What happened? Oh my gosh. Are you okay?" I turn to the paramedics. "Is she okay? How did this happen?"

They shove me back. "I'm sorry, sir. You'll have to stay back."

Janny pulls off her oxygen mask. "Micah!" She reaches out to me.

I rush over and take her hand. "You're safe. You're at the hospital."

She squeezes my hand. "No, Theo! Theo! I don't... you have to find Theo."

Theo. Dear God in Heaven...

They wheel her into trauma, and I'm left standing in the shadows.

I spin around expecting them to wheel in my son on a separate stretcher. But no stretcher comes. They don't have him. He was with her. He had to be with her. However she got like this, he was there too. And they don't have him. They don't know!

Ed rushes to my side and steadies me. I didn't even realize how much I'd started shaking.

Ed takes my head in his hands. "We will find him, Micah."

"I can't lose him too, Ed. I can't..."

Francesco

"Let's go. We'll find out what happened, and we will find him."

I take out my keys, but Ed takes them from me. "No, not like this. I'll drive. Micah, we're not going to lose him." Ed swallows hard and takes a deep breath. "I won't let it happen. Now let's go get your son."

We find out from the paramedics where Janny's car ran off the road. It's by the creek, which in this weather is more ice than creek.

I grip my hands together, cold sweat making them slide. My arms all pound with blood vessels as I picture the worst. Theo in a casket. His name chiseled into our family tombstone. My home, my store, empty of the last remnant of the life I torched with my betrayal.

"I can't lose him, Ed."

"You haven't lost him, Micah. Not yet."

"Why didn't they bring him in with her?"

Ed gets quiet and slowly exhales. "Micah. We can't help Theo by assuming the worst. Right now, you need to pray. That's all we can do until we can get there, until we can find him."

Ed parks and we rush out. I rush to the scene but the police stop me. "Sir, you need to return to your vehicle."

"My son's in that water."

"I assure you, we're doing everything we can to find him. You're not helping him if we have to rescue you too. Let us handle this."

I storm back to Ed's car and pound the hood. "I can't just stand here doing nothing."

Ed looks over the side of the road where rescuers are dragging the waters looking for Theo. "How did they find Janny but not Theo? Maybe he walked away from the wreckage? Have you checked with any local residents or businesses?"

"Sir, we know how to do our job. Please, return to your vehicle. We'll find him."

Ed loads me back into his car. We sit in the piercing silence and all I can hear is my sobs.

Ed puts his hand on my shoulder. "There's nothing we can do here that they aren't doing. They're looking for him. If he's anywhere in this vicinity, they'll find him."

"Ed, it's below 20 degrees out. If they don't find him fast, he won't be alive when they do."

"People have survived much worse temperatures. Have faith, Micah. Pray."

I shake my head and storm out of the car. "You pray. I'm doing."

Ed gets out and chases after me. "Micah!"

I storm the other direction from the crash site. They're looking down stream, but the water is increasingly frozen. If Theo was somehow thrown from the vehicle or walked away on foot, they could be missing him.

I walk down an embankment, looking for any sign of him. A piece of clothing, a footprint in the snow. Even a blood trail. Anything to indicate which way he might've gone.

"Theo!" I call out. A shot in the dark that he can hear me. That he can call back.

The winds and snow seem to pick up at that moment. They pound my face, but I don't care about the pain. I'd suffer for the rest of my life if Theo could just be okay.

I run farther down the shoreline of the creek. I used to play here as a kid. There are hidden coves in the trees. I call out to him again and search a hidden cove of water. Nothing. A part of me relieved, a part of me even more frantic that I still don't know where he is.

Then I see another cove down a few yards. I sprint toward it, catching myself as I slip.

I can barely see anything in the dark, snowy area. But as I squint, I catch what seems to be the outline of a small body in the water. For a split second, I wonder if it's my mind playing tricks on me. The cruel illusion of a winter's night. Then I get closer and I see his face. Theo!

Before I can even make a dash to save him, Ed jumps into the water.

When *Miracles* Can *Dream*

"Ed!" I call out to him, but he's at Theo before I can even react.

He wraps Theo in his arms and drags him ashore.

He's blue.

Dear God in heaven, my son is blue!

My wife and daughter had more color when I saw them in the morgue than he does right now. His eyes are closed and his face covered in frost.

Ed listens for a breath. Nothing.

He checks for a pulse. Still nothing.

He's dead. My little boy. My precious son. He's dead. He's gone forever and I can only sit here watching.

Ed begins to do CPR. "Go flag the paramedics. We have to get him to a hospital. He's not dead. Not yet. We can still save him."

"I can't leave him."

"He is not alone. He needs you to get him help. Trust him to me, Micah. Go get him help."

I take a step back, looking at Theo's face one more time. This may be the last time I see it when he's not declared dead. When there's still supposedly some hope left.

I run to get him help. I think of our last conversation. Every time through the years he reached out to me, and I turned him away. All the time working at our store I just gave him something to do instead of teaching him the business I loved. Now it could be all gone. I'd bury him next to his mother and sister and live the rest of my life alone.

Kelsey. He never even got to meet her. And now she might not even wake up.

Did he suffer? Did he call for me in his last moments? Is he being held by Jesus right now? Or maybe all the faith I was taught was a lie and he's cold and dark in nothingness, his last memories of existence being of my failing him.

My breaths become heavier and harder, but I push through.

I don't even hear the words leaving my mouth as I talk to the paramedics. I feel like I am not even in control of my body anymore. My mind is one place and my body another. Something must have gotten through to them, because they all run in his direction.

The next thing I know, I'm back there with them, and they're all over Theo, attaching him to various devices and compressing his chest. They lift him onto a stretcher and rush him into the back of an ambulance.

They guide Ed and me back to the road.

One of them places a hand on my shoulder and says something. I don't even hear it. But I nod, my body still acting apart from my mind.

I think of a time when Theo was three. We'd just had Melanie and it was Christmas Eve. Christy had gone to bed, but I was still up. Brooding by the fireplace like usual, upset that I couldn't be with both Kelsey and my family for the holiday.

Then I looked up and I saw little pajama feet walking to the kitchen.

"Aren't you supposed to be asleep? Santa won't come if you're awake."

"I didn't put out carrots for the reindeer."

He opened the fridge and took out a big carrot from the veggie drawer. Then he went to get a knife.

I raced to my feet and got there first. "Why don't you let me help you with that?" I grabbed the knife and got out a plate. Guiding his hands very carefully, we cut the carrot up into nine pieces. One for each reindeer. Then we put them on a small plate and set it next to the milk and cookies left for Santa.

"There! Now the reindeer won't be hungry."

I lifted that little toddler in my arms and kissed his forehead. It was one of the few moments of his life I can remember initiating affection with him. I wonder if he remembers it too. I carried him back to bed and tucked him in again, promising him that if he went to sleep, Santa would come soon.

As I stand there watching them load my little boy into the back of an ambulance, I pray to God that somehow, I could go back to that moment and stay there. Choose to be a better father to him. Choose a path that would've never left my only son on a dark road during a snowy Christmas night.

Ed grabs my hand. "Believe God can heal him. When I lost my Toby that night, he was taken from the scene in a body bag. There wasn't any hope left. Theo's in an ambulance. They're going to do everything they can to save him. Trust that they will."

The tears win out and start pouring out of me. "I don't have any trust left. I just don't know how I can live if he dies, Ed. I can't . . ."

Ed pulls me into an embrace and I bury my head on his shoulder. Weeping, so uncontrollably. Like I've never wept before, even after Christy and Melanie died. I had to be strong then. But I have no strength left, nobody left to be strong for.

Ed pats my head a moment and then eases me to my feet. I didn't even realize I'd fallen.

"Let me get you to the hospital. We'll make sure you're there. Whatever happens."

I nod and we turn to go.

Ed freezes in place for a moment.

I turn to him. "Ed?"

He looks at me and I see his eyes turn dark. "Get to Theo."

Then he grabs his chest and sinks to his knees.

I rush to his side and catch him before he hits the ground.

"Ed, oh my gosh. Ed . . . are you?"

I wave to the paramedics. "We need help over here!"

Paramedics rush back to us and get Ed onto a stretcher. They put an oxygen mask on him, and then wheel him into a second ambulance that was at the crash site.

The world starts spinning as windy snow continues to pelt me and I try to process everything I know in life spinning out of control. Then everything goes dark. Dark and cold.

Chapter 14
TJ

A half-eaten triple chocolate birthday cake sits on our kitchen table. It was the last birthday cake Mom ever baked for me. It was so chocolatey. The frosting was so soft and creamy and had little pieces of chocolate all over it and the words "Happy Birthday, T.J." in raspberry. I never tasted another cake as good as that one.

I go up to it and pick up a small chunk that spilled on the table. It still tastes as sweet as the day she baked it for me.

In the other room, I can hear Melanie singing along to that stupid make-up doll commercial. I used to hate that song, and I hated it even more when she would sing her really bad version of it. Now, it just feels great to hear her voice again.

I run into the living room, and I can see her. She's dancing and jumping around, and her hair is swaying in the breeze from the fan. But her face is turned away from me.

"Melanie!"

She doesn't hear me. She doesn't turn around so I can see her face again.

I run up to her, but I pass right through her. She disappears and the music cuts out.

"Melanie!" I circle the room looking for her, but she's nowhere to be found. Even her toys disappear.

"TJ."

Mom!

I spin around. Her face looks the same as it did that night. So warm. Smiling at me. Letting me know without even saying it that she loves me.

I run to her and we hug. The tightest hug I can remember in my life. I try to remember being six again, feeling her long hair reaching down and surrounding me, and her arms squeezing me so tight I felt like nothing else could touch me. I still feel safe in her arms, but now I'm so afraid of letting go. Afraid of not seeing her anymore, of being alone again.

"TJ, you're so loved and so safe. I wish you could believe me."

"I'm trying, Mom. I want to."

But she's already gone. Then our house vanishes too and I'm at Dad's store.

I walk down some of the aisles. The store must be closed. Nobody's here, and the only lights on are the Christmas lights.

I look at the movie scene villages I helped make. When I press the big red button, they play the movie scene over a little speaker. Ralphie comes down in a pink bunny suit. Rudolph leads Santa's sleigh through the storm. Buddy meets his dad at the Empire State Building. I can see myself watching those movies with Mom and Melanie and remember how much I loved helping make this section of the store. It was one of the few times I can remember feeling like Dad was proud of me.

Then I hear a bunch of people yelling.

I look over and I'm in the hospital. I see the doctors in an operating room all standing over someone, doing lots of medical things I don't quite understand. It's like the doctors on TV, but crazier.

I walk over and get between them and see that it's me on the table. I'm blue. Well, not really blue. But not the normal me color either. My skin looks so different.

I see them slide one of my eyes open and look with a flashlight. My eyes look so creepy. Like something out of a scary movie. That's not what my eyes look like!

They let my eyes close again and continue working on me.

I take steps back until I can't see them anymore. I hear myself sobbing, but I can't feel tears on my face.

Am I dead? Did I die? Then why can't I stay with Mom or Melanie? Maybe I don't get to go to heaven like them.

"Mom!" I call out. Silence.

"Dad!" I can't believe I'm calling out for him. But right now, I'd give anything to see him and beg him to hold me and tell me that it was going to be okay.

I look at the heart monitor and see the big flat line going by on the screen. I know from TV that's bad. I'm dead. That's what that means, right? But the doctors are still working on me, so maybe there's still a chance? I don't know. It all looks so scary. When I look closer, they have a tube down my throat and are pressing on my chest.

"Hey!" I scream. I just want someone to see me. So I know I still exist, and I'm not some ghost. But nobody can hear me. Nobody can see me. They all think I'm dead on that table.

I run away. Through one door and then another. Halls and halls that seem to go nowhere and go on forever. Nobody else is here. Just me alone, running through them crying, the loud sound of the machines trying to bring me back to life the only thing in my ears. It's almost worse hearing them than the silence, because each screech reminds me that I'm slipping away. Further and further away.

Then I see Dad. Only older, with gray hair. He's alone, running his store all day. Nobody to love him. Nothing but pictures of all the people he loves who died. Pictures of his mom and dad, of Melanie, of Mom, of the sister I never met. And of me.

Even though it's Christmas Eve night, he stays alone in his store, crying and staring at our pictures, touching them like he's trying to remember what we feel like.

I try to run to him, but everything gets farther and farther away. I chase it, but that just makes it all go faster. Why can't I catch up? I don't want to go. I want

WHEN *Miracles* CAN *Dream*

to make things right with Dad.

I say every prayer I can think of. Prayers I learned in school. Prayers Mom taught me. Prayers I just make up on the spot. Anything. Something to try and tell God how I feel. To stop my mind from spinning and spinning and making me so dizzy. Because I don't want to die. I don't want to leave Dad. I just want things to be good again.

Then things get dark again and everything goes quiet, and it gets hard to think of anything. I try to think of things before I can't anymore. *I love you, Dad. I'm sorry. I just want us to be happy . . .*

Chapter 15
Micah

I never realized how many sounds the hospital has at night. The machines keeping the patients alive. The rattle of carts rolling down the hallways. The footsteps of nurses making rounds to check on patients. Even the flicker of a candle in the chapel.

This hospital chapel can seat about ten people, maybe twenty if everyone squeezes in and some stand. But sitting in here all alone, it might as well be an empty cathedral.

Four people I care about could die tonight. They're all in this hospital fighting just to stay alive. And I can't do a thing to help them. It's been hours since we brought in Theo and Ed. Hours since a doctor has given me any update. For all I know, they could all be in the morgue right now.

I stare at the tiny altar up against the wall of the chapel, a tiny tabernacle sitting above it. I wonder if God can even hear me after barely speaking to Him for years now. Why would He listen to the prayers of someone who caused all of the problems he's asking God to fix? If I had just been a better father, none of them would be in this trouble right now. Theo and Kelsey would be safe at home, warm and probably wrapping Christmas presents. Janny and Ed would be enjoying their own lives free from the consequences of my messed-up life. Maybe if I had died that night instead of Christy. Maybe things would be better.

I replay those horrible scenes in my head. Theo's lifeless body. Ed grabbing his chest and hitting the ground. Janny being wheeled in bleeding. Kelsey spending weeks in a coma. The only thing worse than these images is seeing the ones I fear in my head, their pale lifeless bodies on a slab in a morgue. Like Christy and Melanie were that night.

I try to conjure up some image of hope, something positive. The doctors telling me that everyone is going to pull through this. But I can't seem to make these stay together. They just fall apart into little pieces and dissipate in the scenes of horror replaying over and over again.

The door creaks.

I look up and see a nun's silhouette walking slowly to the front of the chapel. She takes a seat next to me. Sister Olivia. Probably the only friend I have left not a patient in this hospital.

A rosary in one hand, she takes my hand in the other. "Oh Micah, I'm so sorry."

"I didn't think it was possible for the world to fall apart so much at one time and still leave me alive."

She gives my hand a squeeze. "But you are alive. I don't know what's going to happen next, but I know that you are alive. I've been here so many times in my life, praying against the impossible. Praying someone I loved would pull through. Sometimes they did.

When *Miracles* Can *Dream*

Sometimes they didn't. But I know that I never left weaker because of my prayers."

I stare at the altar and wonder how I could ever even stand, let alone become stronger, if my children never wake up again.

"You survived what happened to your wife and your daughter. You will survive this, whatever happens. But remember, whatever will happen hasn't happened yet. So as long as you've got reason to hope, then hope. It's Christmas. This is the season when miracles can become real."

"They were my miracles. All of them. They all gave me something I didn't know I needed. And I think I still didn't know just how much until right now. When I might lose them. But I know it. They were my miracles. Maybe God's taking them away because I didn't use them right."

"That's not how God does things."

"I had so many dreams for how my life would go." I swallow hard and take out a picture of Theo from when he was little. "I had so many dreams for how his life would go. And I wrecked each one of them. If he dies now, what good did being my miracle do for him?"

She turns my head and we lock eyes. "Dreams and miracles aren't judged by the same kind of success we judge things of this world by. They're judged by what you choose to let them do for you on the inside."

Francesco

"Theo had dreams . . . and look what that did for him."

"It might just be what keeps him alive."

As more tears spill out of me, she rests my head on her shoulder and she strokes my hand as we each stare at the flickering light coming from the altar, the hours of the night slowly fading.

"She's asking for you." A nurse waves me toward a hospital room. Janny greets me from her bed with a smile.

I sit down next to her and take her hand. "You had me so worried. I thought I'd lost you too."

"I've dealt with retail customers during Christmas week. No car wreck is going to take me out."

I hear myself chuckle despite the tear rolling down my cheek.

She squeezes my hand. "They told me about Ed. I'm so sorry. And Theo . . . any word?"

I shake my head. "I keep telling myself that no news is good news. If he were dead, they'd have come out to me already. If I haven't seen them, it means they're still fighting. That he's still fighting."

"He's a strong kid. He's survived a lot in his life."

"He has." I think of seeing him in that hospital bed that night. "I have to fight for him. I can't lose him too." I reach in and caress her head. "Or you."

"Micah . . ."

When Miracles Can Dream

"Last night, I thought I'd lost everyone I cared about. My children, my friend . . . you. I don't want to lose more time. I don't want my life to pass waiting to be ready. I've made so many mistakes, and a lot of those mistakes were the relationships I put off. I don't want to put off my life anymore to try and punish myself."

"What are you saying?"

"When all of this is over . . . whatever happens. I want to walk through it with you. If you'll have me."

With tears in her eyes, she nods.

I lift her hand and kiss it. It's cold and clammy, but still soft. And until I hear word on Theo or Kelsey, it's the only hand I want to be holding.

The hallway to the ICU seems endless. Dimmer than the rest of the hospital. All that's missing is a sign saying "Abandon hope, all who enter."

They lead me to Theo's bed. The doctor tells me a long monologue about his condition that barely registers. All I can gather is that we can only wait and see if he wakes up.

They have him hooked up to so many tubes. One even breathes for him, going down his throat. Seeing my boy like this hurts like being hit by a truck. My legs nearly collapse as I fall into the chair next to him.

"Oh Theo." I grab his hand and squeeze it, kiss it. Press it to my face. "I'm sorry. For everything."

Francesco

I close my eyes for a moment and listen to the heart monitor. His heart's still beating. I focus on that steady beat. The doctors said his heart stopped, but they were able to get it beating again. His color's still pale, but better than it was last night.

I stare at his face and stroke some of his auburn curls, praying that he'd open his eyes, and I could spend the rest of my life making up for all the time I wasted with him.

"When you wake up, we'll get a Christmas tree. And decorate the house. We'll do all the things we should've been doing all this time. I'm sorry it took so long for me to figure things out, Theo. I am. If you'll forgive me, maybe we can try again? But we can't do that until you fight. Fight for me, Theo. Come back to Dad."

I lean in and I kiss his forehead. "You were always my miracle, Theo. Don't let things end this way. Give me one more chance to be your father."

I go into Ed's room, each step so hesitant that I nearly fall over trying to hold myself back.

I swallow hard as I take a seat next to him. Somehow he looks thirty years older in the span of a day.

He groans slightly and turns to me. His eyes open and a tear falls out. "Thank you for coming. I know it must've been hard to leave Theo's side. I promise I won't keep you too long."

"It's okay. I think Theo would want me to check in on you."

Ed coughs a moment and I help steady him. He presses his chest and leans back into his pillow. "Did they tell you if Theo's going to make it or not?"

"They don't know yet." My breath shakes as a shiver shoots through every part of me. "They say he's stable, but they say the next twenty-four hours are crucial. They always say that when they don't know, don't they?"

"And Janny?"

"She has a mild concussion, a couple minor cuts and bruises. But they say she'll make a full recovery. She was lucky."

He smiles. "That's good. That's very good. You and Theo will need her to move forward from this."

I chuckle. "Is that a fact?"

"Don't pretend that everyone doesn't see how you two have been dancing around your feelings for one another."

I shake my head. "You should really save your strength. Don't waste it trying to be the love doctor."

Ed laughs. But not his usually jolly bellow. It's a silent, near heave that ends in another coughing fit.

"What did the doctors say about your condition?"

Ed breathes in a heavy breath. "My heart seems to have reached its expiration date. I've taken medication for it for years. This wasn't even my first heart attack."

"You never said anything."

"It's not exactly something that leads conversations very naturally."

"Ed... these past few weeks have been... I've come to view you as a friend. Theo looks at you almost like a grandfather. The customers love you. You've brought so much joy to our lives. You could've told us."

Ed nods. "I suppose I could have. But you all had enough to worry about without needing to worry about some old man. I met you in the midst of your own problems. Helping you even by bringing just a little bit of joy helped me more than your worry could have." He gestures to the table next to his bed. There's an envelope and a wallet on it.

I pick them up and hand them to him.

He pushes them back into my hand. "Micah, I updated my will a few weeks ago. Anything I own, which I admit isn't much, I want you to have. I'm not some secret millionaire. I can't singlehandedly change your life with some miracle inheritance. But you and Theo are the closest things I've had to a family since I lost Toby. When I'm gone, I want you to have anything left of mine."

"Ed, I don't know what to say."

"Don't say anything. Be a father to that boy. That's all I ask of you."

"Ed, I don't even know if he's going to make it."

"Oh he'll make it. I'll make sure of it when I get up there."

I raise an eyebrow. "And who says you're going anywhere?"

Ed pats my arm. "I signed a DNR. Micah, I don't want to fight the inevitable. My heart's been hurting for so long. I've lived a long life. I've done a lot of good things. And hopefully, I've helped some people. Hopefully, I've helped you. I don't need to keep fighting anymore." A tear streams down his cheek. "If I can see my Toby for Christmas this year, that would be the greatest gift the Lord could give me."

I wipe a tear from my eye. "Some days it hurts so much not seeing Christy or Melanie. And the thought of not seeing Theo again for decades just makes my chest hurt. I'm so sorry for everything you've gone through, Ed."

Ed smiles and opens his wallet. He takes out a worn picture. "This is my Toby. Whenever life would begin to hurt, I would take out his picture and look at him. It didn't make the hurt go away. But it did give me something good to hold onto, the hope that I would see him again. And then all the mistakes I ever made would melt away and we could be happy. Forever. He was my miracle. And he didn't stop being my miracle just because he wasn't alive anymore. We're all miracles. Each one of us. And miracles don't stop with this life, Micah. They keep going. Sometimes we just have to wait to see them again. Whatever happens to Theo, he is your miracle. Never let go of that."

Francesco

I take the picture from Ed. It's a picture of him with a little boy around Theo's age. Same dark hair as his father. Ed looks so different with a full head of dark hair and a clean-shaven face. I smile, wondering if this is how Theo and I look to anyone else.

When I look closer, there's something about his son that seems familiar. But I can't place it. Maybe it's just déjà vu? But it feels like more. Something inside of me knows that face, those warm eyes or that gentle smile. It's like the ghost of a memory that I buried so many years ago.

As I stare into that boy's eyes, I recall the last time I stared into those eyes. Just like right now, I was crying. I was terrified. My chest was pounding. Only then, a fire was blazing around me.

"This is your son?"

"That was taken a few months before I lost him."

I run my hands over the worn picture, sweat beads forming on my brow. Ed said his son died in an accident. He never said what that was. Could it be?

"It was a fire, wasn't it? At a Church..."

Ed's eyes go wide. "How could you know that?"

"Because I was there." I sniffle hard and force my weeping face to smile.

"You were there?"

"It was a Church that used to be where St. Matthew's is. We were there for Christmas Eve Mass. I was a little kid so I don't remember how it happened. Just that a fire started. Somehow I got separated from my

When *Miracles* Can *Dream*

parents. The flames got so big and there was so much smoke. Light fixtures were falling, and it was total chaos. I couldn't get out and I was so scared. I found a pew and crawled under it. I was little so I could fit. I thought I was going to die there. But then, somebody reached in and said he was going to help get me out. It wasn't a fireman. It was another kid. A few years older than me. I'll never forget his face or those warm eyes. He said the firemen were on their way, but that it might be too late by then. So he wrapped me in some robe and picked me up. He pressed me close to him so the smoke couldn't get in, and before I knew it . . . we were outside. He set me on the ground, and I could breathe in real air. It felt so good that I cried. My parents found me shortly after and didn't leave my side again. When I told them a kid had saved me, they thought I was just traumatized. Or maybe that it was my guardian angel. I never saw him again after that, even though our town is so small. I started to think maybe they were right. But they weren't, were they? That was your son who saved me . . . Toby."

Ed begins to cry, but a smile eases onto his face. "That's my boy. He had the kindest heart. Even putting his own life in danger just to help another person. That night, the witnesses said they saw him running into the building several times and helping people get out. When the firefighters finally got there, he was collapsed by the altar. They pulled him out and tried to resuscitate him. But it was too late. He'd taken in too much smoke. He was gone. But even though they said he shouldn't have gone back in, they said more people probably would have died if he hadn't gotten them out. Many of them children. It was Christmas Eve, so everyone was there with their families. I wasn't there. I was working. Maybe if I had been there . . . I could've gotten him out. He got out almost ten people, but I wasn't there to get *him* out." Ed's cries get harder and deeper.

I embrace him tightly. "You can't blame yourself for that. It was a fire. Toby sounds like he was going to help as many people as he could, no matter what. He saved my life. If it weren't for him, I wouldn't be alive. Theo would've never even been here. I can never do anything to repay him for what he gave me."

Ed takes my hand. "Yes you can. You can love your son. You can seize your life right now, because regardless of any time you've wasted, you still have one. Take back your family, Micah. And never let them go. That's how you can honor my Toby."

I nod and return the picture to Ed.

"Keep it." He pushes it gently to me. "I'd like it if there were someone else to remember him when I'm gone."

I nod and put it in my pocket. "I'll never forget him. And I'll never stop thanking him."

Ed looks up at the ceiling. "Do you think I'll see him again, Micah? It's been so long that I forget what his voice sounds like. How could I forget my own little boy's voice?"

I hear Ed's heart monitor begin to ramp up. I take his hand in mine and squeeze it tighter. "Just listen. Listen closely and you'll hear him. He's probably calling to you right now. He's waiting for you. He's missed his daddy."

Ed's cries turn into a laugh and then a cough. "Go to your son, Micah. I'm going to go see mine."

And just like that, he closes his eyes and exhales a final extended breath.

My insides sink as I see my friend go limp. I let go of his hand and it falls gently to his side.

The nurses come in and turn off the monitor after a moment, and I'm just left standing there with my emotions hanging there raw.

Chapter 16
TJ

I open my eyes to the flickering of candles. Almost an endless stream of them! The smell of incense and the sound of chanting help my chest stop pounding so much. I can finally take a breath.

It's that little Church I met Marcus at. It's all decorated for Christmas now, the best Christmas decorations I've ever seen. The lighted garland hangs everywhere from the ceiling to each pew. Under each Station of the Cross, they have a wreath hanging. And a thousand million poinsettias line the altar. And the Nativity Scene at the front has the most beautiful statue collection I've ever seen. The statues look almost real.

I look around and see lots of people in the Church, sitting quietly reading the Missal or kneeling in prayer.

I wonder if maybe I'm dead and this is heaven. Maybe like seeing my house or Dad's store, this is just my brain using my memories to help me figure things out. Maybe Jesus is going to walk out any second and tell me I'm dead.

"No, TJ. You're not dead." That voice. So familiar.

I look up and everyone's gone.

Then I look over and see Marcus at the altar, dressed in his altar server robe.

"Marcus! What are you doing here?" I swallow hard. "Are you even really here? Am I really here?"

Francesco

He smiles and lets out a chuckle. "That depends on what you mean by real. Yes, this is real, but no, we're not physically in this building in the same way you're thinking. Right now, you're in a hospital and the doctors are trying to make you better."

"Wait, I'm in a hospital?"

He nods. "Twisted ankle, then car crash, dip in the freezing creek. Ring a bell?"

I try to think back and remember, but it's all moving so fast. It's like a movie speeding by on fast forward, and everything is just flashing in my head. I don't know what's real and what's a dream.

"I don't know. I'm so confused." I hold my head and try to focus.

Marcus walks over and moves my hands down. "You don't have to be afraid, TJ."

I look into his eyes. They are warm and friendly. I feel my worry slowly going away.

"But if I'm here because I'm in the hospital . . . why are *you* here?"

He takes a deep breath. "We should talk."

Then I hear the doors to the Church swing open.

Marcus looks up and smiles. "Hi, Dad. It's good to see you again."

I turn around and see Mr. Gabriel standing in the back of the Church. He's dressed like Santa and looks a little bit confused. He walks up the center aisle slowly, his shoes clanking on the marble floors.

When Miracles Can Dream

"Toby." His lips slowly move into a smile. "It's really you, isn't it?"

Marcus runs to Mr. Gabriel with a smile and open arms.

Mr. Gabriel sweeps him off the floor and into an air hug. Tears spill down their faces, but they look like happy tears.

Mr. Gabriel pulls Marcus back and kisses his forehead. "Toby, I've waited so many years to see you . . . to hear you again."

Marcus smiles. "I know. I've been watching. You don't have to cry anymore, Dad. For the rest of forever, we're going to be a family again."

He leads Mr. Gabriel to the altar.

I take a step back. "I don't understand."

Mr. Gabriel looks up at me. "TJ . . . you're here. Does this mean . . . ?"

Marcus puts out his hand and shakes his head. "No. TJ can still go back."

Mr. Gabriel walks over to me and kneels down. "I'm so sorry, TJ. We should've found you sooner."

"But . . . if I'm the one who got hurt, why are you here too?"

He steps back and goes to Marcus. "My heart's been sick for a long time. It just couldn't get better this time."

"So you're dead?" My eyes fill with tears.

Mr. Gabriel wipes one off my cheek. "Don't be sad for me, TJ. I'm back with my little boy. I couldn't be any happier. But you have a father too who's praying for you to come back to him. You can't let him down."

I look to Marcus. "I don't understand any of this. Like, I understand how Mr. Gabriel is here, and I guess I get why I'm here. But why are you here? If Mr. Gabriel's son hasn't been alive for a long time, how could you be him? We've were hanging out even before I got hurt."

Marcus tucks his hands behind his back. "These past few weeks . . . it's been great getting to be your friend. But things haven't exactly been the way you've seen them." He looks around the Church. "A long time ago, like when your dad was a little boy, this Church here stood near where St. Matthew's is today. It was a nice little Church that the people of this town all cherished. But things were changing in the world back then. Not everyone liked older Churches like ours or what they had to say in them about certain things like the sins people liked to do. And someone decided to do something very bad one Christmas Eve night. They came in and turned over some of our candles in a side room where nobody could see them. That way, by the time anyone noticed there was a fire, it was too late to put it out. The fire spread so quickly. A lot of people were able to get out, but a lot of people weren't. Your dad was one of the ones trapped in here by the fire."

"My dad was here? But if he was trapped, how did he get out?"

When Miracles Can Dream

Marcus looks down and kicks his feet together. "I was helping to get people out. I saw him hiding underneath a pew and knew that by the time the firemen would find him, it would be too late. So I went and got him and carried him outside."

I remember hearing Dad say something about this, but I never imagined it happened here.

"But . . . if you got him out, why didn't you grow up like him?"

He sighs. "I went back in to help more people, but I breathed in too much smoke. And the doctors couldn't get me back. I died that night, TJ."

I shake my head and take a step back. "No. You can't be dead. You couldn't have been dead all this time. I met you here. I saw you in my store. Other people saw you."

"Are you sure about that? Think back."

I replay all of our meetings. Could I really be the only one who saw him? "But I went to your house. I met your mom. We ate pizza from a restaurant. We wrestled. I felt your body with my own hands. You can't be some ghost."

"Like I said TJ, just because it wasn't happening the way you thought doesn't mean it wasn't real. Physically, those things didn't happen the way that other things you experienced happened. But they were still real. To you."

"So all of that was just in my head?"

"I would say more in your heart. This church burned down over thirty years ago. But sometimes, those who need it can still find it. Like you did."

I see Marcus's mother walk out from behind the altar.

"Hi, TJ. It's good to see you."

She walks over to Mr. Gabriel and throws her arms around him. "I know you've spent your life feeling guilty about the mistakes you made with our son, but you raised a kind and strong person. I couldn't be prouder of who he is. I see you still call him by his middle name all these years later."

Mr. Gabriel kisses her and hugs her tighter. He doesn't say anything else, but somehow I know exactly what he's thinking.

Marcus takes me aside. "Are you okay? I know this is a lot."

"A lot? I'm just finding out that my new friend is dead. And he's been dead for years. No, I'm not okay."

He sighs and pats me on the back. "I know. And I can't just make this all make sense."

"Why did I see you, though? Even before I got hurt?"

"Now that I live in heaven, God has me help people who need it. You needed help. You were sad. You were angry. You were letting those bad feelings hurt your life. You needed to find this Church. You needed a friend who would listen to you. I tried to be that friend. I hope I was able to help at least a little."

Tears spill out and I nod. "You were the first real friend I had in a long time. I don't want you to go away. Is this why you said you and your mom were moving on? Because I'm never going to see you again?"

He shakes his head. "We use that word a lot, 'never.' Heaven might be a long time away, but it's not 'never.'" He looks over to Mr. Gabriel. "It took all of his life, but for my dad, he's finally getting the things it seemed like he'd never get to see again." He smiles at me. "You'll see me again. But for the time being, we have to be apart. You have to go and live. Really live. It's time, TJ."

I throw my arms around him and hug him tight. He feels so real in my arms. I can feel the bones of his shoulders and arms. I can hear him breathing. How can he just be some spirit in my "heart"? How can he really have been dead all this time?

Marcus pats my back and takes a step back. "You have things you need to do. Good things. Things to help people. And even normal, simple, stupid everyday things. Things that will make you happy." He fist bumps me. "And I'm not going to stop looking out for you just because you can't see me anymore. Just like I never stopped looking out for my dad."

I turn to Mr. Gabriel. I stare at his face and take a step to him. "You were the one who pulled me out of the house that night, weren't you? I kept thinking I was crazy this whole time, but it was really you."

Francesco

He gets quiet and nods. "I didn't think you remembered."

"Why didn't you say something? We could've thanked you better."

"I didn't want you to think of me any differently. I didn't even realize it at first myself. You've grown up so much since then. By the time I did figure it out, I didn't want you and your father to feel like you owed me. I didn't do anything spectacular. I was making a delivery to a house in your neighborhood that night, and I saw your mother pass out through the window. Something inside me told me to intervene and so I did. I was just in the right place at the right time that night. I guess my Toby was just taking after me in trying to help strangers, huh?" He nudges Marcus.

"You saved me again tonight, didn't you? That's why you died?"

"I died because it was my time, TJ. It's not your time tonight."

The three of them walk toward the altar.

Marcus points to the door. It opens gently. The snow's slowed to a gentle flurry. "It's time, TJ. It's time to go back."

"I don't know if I'm ready."

Marcus turns to me. "You're readier than you think. Don't wait any longer to be happy, TJ."

Mr. Gabriel taps me on the shoulder. "Remember what I said about being Santa. Being Santa is about what you do for others, not about fitting some silly profile. You can be Santa for someone else, TJ. Every day of your life."

They all hug me goodbye and then stand together at the foot of the altar. Mr. Gabriel seems to be getting younger. He looks a lot like Marcus as his hair turns brown again.

"Thank you," I say. Then I turn to the doors and take a step outside, trying to take in the moment. Remember how the Church smells of incense, the sounds of monks chanting in the background. The voices of my friends wishing me well. The feeling inside that I'm safe, the first time since Mom died I can ever remember feeling safe. I don't want to ever forget this moment as long as I live.

Then I open my eyes.

Chapter 17
Micah

It was like God Himself reached down and stopped my world from flying out of control the moment I saw Theo open his eyes again.

The nurses warned me not to get excited if he did. It could just be a reflex. But I could see it in the way he looked at me. He was back.

"Hey there, kiddo. Welcome back."

I paged his medical team to come in. Before long, they were able to get him off the tubes. I couldn't believe it. His color was back. He was able to breathe and sit up on his own. Even the doctors were amazed by how quickly he'd gone from death's door to barely injured at all. He complained more about his twisted ankle than he did anything else.

When we were alone again, I took my place next to him and cradled his hand in mine. "Do you know how much I love you? I thought I'd lost you. For good this time. Theo, I'm so sorry. For all the times I failed you, which has probably been every day of your life. I know we have a lot to work through, but I don't want to hide from those tough conversations anymore. I don't want to put off being your father another day."

Theo's eyes tear up, but he doesn't say anything.

"It's okay. We don't have to talk yet. You focus on getting better."

Francesco

Theo sits up a bit in his bed. "Dad, there's so much I need to tell you. So much that I saw."

I wipe away one of his tears. "And you will tell me. And I'll listen. But don't worry about that tonight. I almost lost you. When we pulled you out of that water, I thought you were dead. I think you might've actually been dead. And yet now you're here, talking to me. I spent the past 36 hours thinking I was going to be burying my son in a few days. Now, on Christmas Eve, I get you back. I get another chance. And I don't want to throw that chance away on anything. I know we have a lot to talk about. But for right now, I just want to enjoy the holiday, and start fresh right here on setting our lives right."

"Dad, I'm sorry."

I pull him into a hug, stroking his hair and pulling him so close, I can hear his heart beating. It's the sweetest sound I ever heard. "We both are, kiddo."

The picture of Ed and his son falls out of my pocket.

Theo sees it and points. "What's that?"

I pick it up and show him. "Like I said, there's a lot we'll have to talk about later."

He takes it and runs his hands across the picture. "It really is him."

I start to ask him what he means by that, but I guess it's one of the things he wants to tell me. He did almost die. Maybe he already knows about a lot of this anyway.

When Miracles Can Dream

"Hey, I know it's not Christmas just yet, but I wanted to give you your present a little early," I say.

He raises an eyebrow. "A present? When did you buy me a present?"

I chuckle. "I own a Christmas store. I had one of the guys drop it off."

I go over to the corner of the room and pull over several large wrapped boxes.

Theo's smile goes wide and he starts laughing. "There's so many."

I pick up the biggest one and place it next to him on his bed. "Yes, there's a lot of them."

I help him tear into the paper until the whole box is uncovered.

"It's a Christmas tree!" His eyes go wide.

"Just a small fiber optic one. I promise next year, we'll get you a huge one that will go to the ceiling. But since you're going to be here for Christmas, I figured we can get by with this one for just this year."

He smiles and runs his hands across the box. "It's beautiful."

"You know it looks better out of the box."

He laughs and opens the top flap.

I help him pull the tree out of the box. It's bigger than I expected and stands almost as tall as Theo. We set it on a table next to his bed.

"Now I got permission from the hospital to do this. I hope they don't take it back." I plug in the tree in a spare outlet and turn it on. The room becomes aglow with different colored lights that change from one color to the next.

Theo's eyes glow with the same sparkle as the tree's as he marvels at the lights. It's almost like it's the first Christmas tree he's ever seen.

"I love it, Dad." A tear comes to his eye. "It's awesome."

"And we're not done yet." I pull out more wrapped boxes.

"There's more?"

"We have a lot of Christmases to make up for."

The next one is a string of lights. And then another. We wrap them around the sides of Theo's bed.

Then a box of garland. I string it along the perimeters of the room and make the whole place look like a part of the Christmas village at my store.

Then a reindeer that sings Christmas carols. Theo presses the button and the thing dances to "Jingle Bells" and "Deck the Halls" and about five other songs. I can understand after the third one why parents hate these things. But Theo loves it and so I'm going to put up with it.

Theo opens the next one and gets quiet. It's a bin full of old decorations from home. The stockings he used with Christy and Melanie that last Christmas, some keepsake ornaments from our old tree, and other various Christmas knickknacks.

Theo takes each one and presses it against his chest, closing his eyes and probably trying to picture the last time he saw each thing. A time when he still had his mother and sister. A time before he realized how much I was going to let him down.

"Dad, this is everything I've wanted for so long. It's like Mom and Melanie are here again." He sniffles and hangs one of the ornaments on the tree.

I take others and we fill the tree so not a branch is left without an ornament on it.

I sit down on the bed next to him and put my arm around him. "I really hope the doctors don't freak when they come in and see what 'a couple of Christmas decorations' looks like."

"Just tell them it makes me feel better and that I'll fall back into a coma without them."

I laugh and ruffle his hair. Then I lean down and kiss his forehead.

We both look up at the Christmas wonderland we've turned his hospital room into.

Seeing the colored lights reflecting in his wonder-filled eyes is probably the best image I have seen since I held him and his sister for the first time as babies. For the first time since I can remember, all of the guilt and regret just slips away, and I feel a lightness in my chest that I can only imagine must be what true joy feels like.

"Can we play some Christmas music?" he asks.

"Sure thing, kiddo." I take out my phone and call up the local Christmas radio app.

An instrumental Christmas song begins to play.

"Mannheim Steamroller!" Theo's voice has a mix of playful shouting and subtle quiet that only a kid can ever produce. "Mom played them that night. It was the last Christmas music we heard together." He cries again, but he knocks my hand away when I try to dry his tears. "No, I want these tears. I want to remember them. Hearing this song makes it feel like we're all together."

I stroke his head and pull him close, feeling the warmth of his body in my arms and reflecting for a moment how cold he was when I pulled him out of that water. And how close I came to never feeling his warmth again.

"Thank you, Dad," he says. "I wish I could've gotten you something. You did so much. More than I ever could've dreamed of. It's all so beautiful. And I don't have anything to give you."

"You did give me a gift this year," I say. "A better gift than anything anyone could've gotten me." I snuggle him just a little closer. "You came back to me."

Chapter 18
TJ

When I open my eyes on Christmas morning and see all of the Christmas lights Dad and I hung last night, it feels like I must be in heaven. Of all the lights I've seen in our store and around town, these are the prettiest. It almost doesn't even look like I'm in a hospital room anymore. It's more like a Christmas wonderland.

I look over and see Dad asleep in the chair next to me. He must be so tired after worrying for these past few days. Then again, it seems like he's been worrying for a lot of years now. Keeping secrets, missing Mom and Melanie. Maybe now that he's finally got all of that off his back, he can rest easy.

I take out the picture Dad had of Mr. Gabriel and Marcus. I can't believe that Mr. Gabriel was Marcus's dad this whole time. Even crazier that Marcus and his mom were both dead the whole time. All of the things we did together were like a vision, I guess. I don't quite understand how it all works. We ate together. We played together. But I guess I don't have to understand how God works. They helped me when I needed it, and so I am grateful.

I feel the faintest breeze sweep through the room. It's weird because there's no door or window open.

I look in my lap and see another picture that wasn't there before. It's the picture Marcus and his mom took at our Baby Jesus party. They both dressed up as angels. I guess they really didn't get a real picture taken. Maybe the angels thing should've been a clue. But the picture is real and it's really in my hand, I think. I want to wake Dad up and ask him if he can see it, but I'm afraid the picture will disappear if I do. And even if it's not real, I can see it. Seeing it makes me happy. That's all I need to know.

Behind it is another picture. This one of me and Marcus playing. I don't even remember when this picture was taken. If they were really physically there, I would've said it had to have been Marcus's mom that took it. We look so happy playing together. I press the pictures close to me and remember what it felt like to be with them. Maybe I'll just keep these pictures for myself for as long as I have them. They can be like my little memories of them.

After the doctors come in and wake Dad up, they look me over and check my breathing. They say it's almost like I was never in that water at all. Even my ankle seems to be feeling a lot better today. They've never seen anything like it. Maybe I'm crazy, but I can almost hear Marcus giggling in my head.

They say that in another day or two, I can probably go home. They just want to keep me a little longer so they can make sure I'm really not going to fall over dead.

When Miracles Can Dream

After the doctors leave, Janny knocks on the door and hobbles in on crutches. "Hey guys, I hope you don't mind a visitor."

"No, not at all," Dad says with a smile.

"They're releasing me today," she says. "Looks like I'm going to pull through." She sits on the edge of my bed. "Seems you're doing better, TJ."

I nod. "Look at what Dad did to my room last night." I point to all the amazing decorations we hung.

She looks around in wonder at all of my Christmas things. "They're beautiful, TJ." She looks over to Dad. "I'm proud of you, Micah. You did a really good thing." She leans over and plants a kiss on his cheek. Dad blushes. I try not to "ewwww," but I think my face does it anyway. I guess maybe now that Dad is letting himself be happy, maybe Janny will finally think about going out with him. I know both of them have wanted to do that for a long time now. She seems like a nice person, and I think Mom would want Dad to be happy again.

I think she even would've forgiven him for becoming Kelsey's dad.

Kelsey. I hadn't even thought about her in all of this. She must still be here in the hospital.

"Dad?"

"Yeah, bud?"

"Can I see her?"

"See who?"

Francesco

"Kelsey. If it's okay, I'd like to meet her. She is my sister. I think Mom would want me to be a good brother to her."

Dad gets quiet for a moment, and his mouth hangs open. Then he takes a deep breath and gets up from the chair. "You got it, bud. I'll take you to see her right now."

Kelsey's room seems so dark after seeing how mine looks decked up in Christmas lights.

Miss Ally sits by her side, gently holding her little girl's hand and whispering prayers through tears.

She turns to us. "Micah . . . you brought Theo."

I walk to Miss Ally and hug her. "I wanted to meet my sister. And say sorry to you for treating you wrong."

"You have nothing to apologize to me for."

"Can I sit with her?"

She nods and wipes tears aside. "I think she would like that."

I walk over to the bed and see Kelsey lying so still. It feels weird thinking that someone with a different skin color is my sister, but when I take her hand in mine, it feels right. I can feel that we're family.

I climb up on the bed next to her and gently stroke her cheek. "Hi Kelsey. My name is Theo. But you can call me TJ. I'm your brother."

I look at Dad standing at the doorway of the room. He's crying too now.

When Miracles Can Dream

I turn back to Kelsey. "I know we haven't met before, and I'm sorry about that. Because I think we would've had a lot of fun. We have another sister who lives in heaven. Her name is Melanie. I think she would've liked you a lot. And you would've liked her too. She loved to dance. She could dance to anything. Sometimes, she would get up and dance in front of everyone. Even total strangers. She wasn't embarrassed or anything. And she would get you to dance with her too. Even if you were scared, you would start having fun when you were with her. I wish you got to meet her. One day you will. But not yet, because we still need you here. We need you to wake up and come back to us. I know I may not be the best brother sometimes. But I know that you're my sister, and I'm your brother. And I know I already love you. So you have to wake up so we can meet the right way. I came back this Christmas. But I think there's still room for another miracle. I don't think they sent me back to watch you in a coma. I think they sent me back so I could get to be your brother. So that means you have to come back, too. You have to wake up."

First it's a tiny squeeze of my hand. So small that I almost feel like it was all in my head. But then I feel it again, and I shoot my eyes to hers.

As if by magic, Kelsey opens her eyes. I can hear everyone in the room gasp.

She turns to me and looks me over. "You're TJ. I saw you in my pictures."

I take her hand and give it a small kiss. "Yeah, I'm TJ."

She sits up a little and a big grin comes onto her face. "I always wanted to meet you."

I smile. "Well, I'm glad we finally could get to meet. I'm sorry it took so long."

Miss Ally cries and runs to Kelsey and hugs her. "My baby. I was so scared."

"I'm sorry I scared you, Mommy." Kelsey hugs her. Seeing them hug, it almost feels like I've known them all my life. Their love feels so right and so real.

I get down from the bed to let Kelsey hug her mom more.

Janny goes to get the doctors.

I walk to dad, and he pats me on the shoulder. "I should've known you would be the one to call her back to us. Theo, I'm sorry that I kept her from you. It was a mistake. I know I betrayed you and your mother by what I did, but Kelsey deserved to know all of her family. It wasn't her fault what I did. It was mine. She should've gotten to know you sooner."

I shrug. "She'll get to know me now. Maybe that's why all of this happened. So we all could start being a family."

Dad smiles and hugs me, and we go to hug Kelsey too.

She giggles and starts singing Christmas songs. So I start singing them with her.

Chapter 19
Micah

December 24. One Year Later.

I tighten the bow of my tux and exhale a hard breath. I'm really doing this.

"It's great that you love Christmas now, but getting married on Christmas Eve is still just a little bit insane." Ed's voice in my head. I wish he were here. He would've loved to see this.

Ed didn't have any family to claim his body. So I did. Theo, Janny, and I were his family. We arranged for him to be buried next to his wife and son.

Theo spent a lot of time staring at the tombstone for Ed's son. Marcus Tobias Gabriel. Theo told me something about seeing Ed's son, but I still can't quite wrap my head around all of that. But the way he stared at that tombstone and ran his fingers across the grooves radiated a painful sadness that I knew was genuine. I just wish I could understand it so I could help him.

Ed had a little more money to his name than he let on. The estate he left us wasn't a millionaire's, but it definitely helped me reinvest in the store. The store's doing better than ever. This year, we had a tribute to Ed placed in the store. A memorial plaque commemorating the time we shared with him. It's a small gesture, but one I think he would've appreciated.

Francesco

We did the Baby Jesus Birthday Party again. It was an even bigger success than last year. We thought of hiring someone else to play Santa, but it felt like nobody could properly fill Ed's boots. Instead, Theo got the idea that he could dress up as Santa and Kelsey could be his elf. Nobody would think he was Santa, but he's really embraced Ed's motto of anyone being Santa. I think customers respond well to it too. Instead of lining up for a photoshoot, Theo goes through the store interacting with them. Even if his lanky form doesn't much resemble Santa, somehow I think he embodies everything Ed thought truly mattered in the role.

Theo's grown so tall in the past year. His voice is still lagging behind, but dang. He's almost as tall as I am. I can't believe how close I came to losing him, how close I came to never getting to see him grow up. I missed out on so much of his life. Not because I wasn't there, but because I wasn't *there*. But Janny has reminded me I can't live in the past. Right now is all that matters, and right now is wonderful. Every day, I become prouder of the young man he's becoming.

"You nervous, Dad?" He comes up to look at me in the mirror. I straighten the bow on his tux and give his hair a ruffle. "After last year, all of this is a piece of cake."

Theo grins and adjusts his cufflinks. "Janny looks really pretty."

When *Miracles* Can *Dream*

I chuckle. "I wouldn't know. I've been locked out of her room since yesterday."

"You sure you don't mind me being your best man? It's not too late to pick someone who's old enough to be like a legal witness."

I give him a playful shove. "We have Ally to be the legal witness. You're the only man I'd ever want standing up for me, Theo."

"I'm not even twelve yet, Dad. I don't think you can say I'm a man."

"Maybe not yet, but you're a lot closer than you think."

I stare into his eyes, and I can see his mother staring back. He smiles and we hug. And I thank God that I'm able to have this moment with him.

It's not even noon yet, but the only way I could get approval to use St. Matthew's for the wedding on Christmas Eve was to make the wedding early. Father kind of laughed at the whole idea of having a wedding on Christmas Eve, but he agreed to do it. A part of me didn't want to use a day with such heavy meaning to start my new life with Janny, but somehow it also felt appropriate to mark the start of my new life with her on this day that has marked the ends and beginnings of so many points in my life. It was time to use this day to set things right.

Francesco

We helped pay for this year's decorations for the Church. The altar has so many poinsettias, I am surprised we have room to stand. We covered the wall behind the altar with gold stars and lit Christmas trees under the stained-glass windows. And garland hung pretty much everywhere from the walls of the Church to the pews. It looks like we're getting married in an official Christmas Church. And I wouldn't have it any other way.

Theo's blowing my mind right now. He's taken on a management role here I didn't even ask him to. He walks around the Church straightening decorations and floral displays, making sure everything is perfect. He definitely has his mother's decorative touch.

The door opens and Ally wheels Phyllis into the Church. She smirks at me and waves her cane.

I walk to her with a smile and open arms and embrace her. "I'm so happy you could make it."

"I wouldn't miss this for the world," she says. "Getting to see you finally sever ties with the family."

I chuckle. Sick burn. She slaps my arm in a playful way, just in case my dense self didn't get her joke. Typical Phyllis. I've missed our little banter.

"Thank you for bringing her," I say, giving Ally a hug.

"Of course." She hugs back. "I'm happy for you, Micah. I really am. It's been a long time coming to finally see you happy again."

"Yes. Yes it has. I'm happy that you can be a part of it."

She shrugs. "Well, Janny has been the best friend to me this past year that I've ever had. I'm in this for her as much as for you."

"Fair enough."

I guess with that, we're ready to start. It's a small wedding, but I like it this way. The people who really matter are here, or are looking down on us.

Sister Olivia gets her camera ready to capture every moment.

Everyone takes their place. And then the music starts. Pachelbel's Canon. And my insides knot with every emotion I've ever felt. Joy, anticipation, memories, regret, fear, hope, pride, love.

The back doors open and Theo walks in with Kelsey on his arm. Both smile as big as the sky as they walk down the center aisle. Kelsey's dark pine green dress looks so Christmassy and highlights her eyes so well.

Theo holds her arm almost like he's her protector. I flash to every moment this past year I've seen them together and how Theo has grown into the best caretaker I've ever seen a kid become.

When they get to the altar, Kelsey goes to the bride's side, and Theo stands by my side.

I clap him on the back and we hug. "Thank you for being here, Theo."

Francesco

He smiles back. "Of course, I'm here. You're my dad."

And for once in my life, I finally feel like I am his father. For real.

Ally follows next, wearing a dress similar to Kelsey's. Kelsey meets her halfway down the aisle and accompanies her to the altar.

Then I see Janny.

And she's beautiful. Subtle white dress, less poofy and glitzy than Christy's was. But still so beautiful and the joy seems to radiate from her flowing red hair. Gold lace highlights her dress and bouquet as she slowly walks down the aisle and makes her way to me.

And then, everything that was broken in my life finally seems to be mended.

Chapter 20
TJ

One Year Later.

I'm twelve and a half years old, but when Christmas comes, I still believe in Santa Claus.

December 25 and the sun isn't even up yet. Every house in town left their Christmas lights on all night. So everything looks like a Christmas wonderland.

When I was little, Christmas was a time of magic. It wasn't just the gifts. Everything seemed to come together to make the world seem like a place of wonder. The colored lights glowing against a snowy night sky. The smell of pine needles or of dough frying in the kitchen. The music of songs that seemed to know just the right notes to play to make the world feel like Christmas.

When I was six years old, my mom and sister died on Christmas Eve. And then the holiday became darker and darker each year as the memories of the good times grew fainter and fainter.

Still, somehow, the feeling of when I was little remained an illusion I chased after every year. I tried everything I could to get back those feelings, even though nothing else in life seemed to be going right.

Two years ago, I met some people who finally helped me get there. They're gone now, but they've made things better with the people I do have in my life. And it seemed, at one of the darkest points in my life when I almost died myself, everything seemed to become right again. Christmas got its magic back.

Last year, Dad got remarried. Janny is a good woman. She's tried her best to be a good stepmom to me without ever trying to make me forget Mom. She had a baby last night. A little boy. They named him Edward Tobias Trader. We're already calling him little Eddie. He's named after two people who really helped us when we needed it. People who deserve to be honored.

I bring my sister Kelsey to visit the ward in the hospital with the new babies. We watch from the outside and wave to him as he sleeps and fidgets in his little blue baby cap.

Then I change into a Santa suit and Kelsey into an elf suit, and we go to the children's wing of the hospital. Kelsey holds a bag of wrapped toys from our store.

We go to the first room. A boy with no hair sleeps in the hospital bed, with the lights of machines where Christmas lights should be.

A woman who must be his mother sits by his side, taking his hand and crying.

"Merry Christmas," Kelsey and I say.

The woman looks up, and her mouth hangs open like she doesn't know what to say.

"We have some gifts for him." Kelsey takes out a wrapped box from the bag.

"I don't understand," she says.

When *Miracles* Can *Dream*

"Just because you're in the hospital doesn't mean you should miss Christmas. What's his name?"

"Timmy. We call him Timmy."

I take out a small Christmas tree.

Timmy wakes up and looks us over. The brightest smile ever comes across his face. I plug in the tree. It lights up, and his eyes get so bright reflecting the different colored lights.

His mom cries and takes her little boy's hand.

"Is this for me?" Timmy sits up in his bed.

I nod. "Santa sent us."

"I didn't think Santa could find me in the hospital."

I shake my head. "Someone once taught me that anyone can be Santa when you choose to do something nice for someone. That's how Santa can find you anywhere."

Kelsey hands Timmy a wrapped gift. "This is for you."

Timmy takes the gift and presses it to his chest and starts laughing. "Santa came, Mom! Santa really came."

She nods and cries and mouths "thank you" to me.

"Can I open it, Mom?"

"Of course."

Kelsey and I wave goodbye and Timmy waves back as he starts to open his present. It's a talking Pikachu. Just like the one I wanted when I was his age.

"It's just what I asked Santa for in my letter." He closes his eyes, presses it to his chest, and hugs it close.

Francesco

"Thank you, Santa," he says.

"Merry Christmas, Timmy," I say as I wave bye and leave with Kelsey.

We go down the hall and do the same thing to the next room until we've given gifts to all the kids there today.

After the last kid, I see the sun coming up through the hospital window. I wipe a tear from my eye, missing for just a moment all the people who I can't see anymore. "Merry Christmas, everyone."

I take out one last gift from the bag and hand it to Kelsey with a kiss on her forehead.

She smiles wide and clutches it close and kisses me. Then runs to find Dad to open it with him.

I swing my sack over my shoulder and watch until she disappears around a corner.

As I follow her down the hall, I can't help but feel like they're walking beside me. Melanie, Mom, Mr. Gabriel, Marcus. Watching with a smile. Wishing me a blessed Christmas. If I close my eyes, I can almost hear the sounds of my last Christmas with Mom or the peaceful chants of that Church.

I think about all the times I sat alone in the dark, wishing for the life I have now. Praying for a miracle. And somehow, I got it. But I never realized that the miracles I wanted weren't things or wishes. They were the people I loved. Friends. Family. They were all my miracles.

When *Miracles* Can *Dream*

I know a lot of these kids in the hospital right now might be thinking the same things I used to. Maybe, at least for one day, I can be a little miracle for them.

I stop a moment and listen. It's quiet, but I can hear it. The sounds of children and parents laughing together. The sound of joy. The sound of hope. It must be what a miracle sounds like.

Acknowledgements

Many thanks to the good folks who helped to give me covid back over Christmas of 2020. It gave me a window to finally sit down and write again during my quarantine. I would likely not have started a new book without that downtime. Also many thanks to the writers and actors through the years who helped inspire a love of Christmas stories in me.

To my love Lulu, thanks for helping give some extra eyes and encouragement to the revisions of this. Thanks for loving a crazy gringo writer. Love Lu.

Thanks to my honorary big sis, Gina Marinello-Sweeney, for always being a sage source of ideas, inspiration, and randomness. Thanks to Mabel Paige for being a crucial early beta reader, and anyone in my circle who gave input at one point or another in the revision process. And of course, thanks again to Jansina for once again turning a scattered author's disjointed ramblings into something beautiful. Thanks to the support of my family, and always to God for giving me a nagging and persistent love of story.

More by J.J. Francesco

Because of Austin

J.J. Francesco

Contact the Author

www.facebook.com/jjfrancesco
www.twitter.com/jjfrancesco

Rivershore Books

www.rivershorebooks.com
blog.rivershorebooks.com
forum.rivershorebooks.com
www.facebook.com/rivershore.books
www.twitter.com/rivershorebooks
Info@rivershorebooks.com

Made in the USA
Middletown, DE
28 October 2022